P9-DNA-441

The Talent Show

DISCARDED

WAYNE PUBLIC LIBRARY

NOV 1 3 2012

Also by Dan Gutman

· ·

The Talent Show

DAN GUTMAN
AUTHOR OF
The
HOMEWORK MACHINE

Simon & Schuster Books for Young Readers
New York   London   Toronto   Sydney   New Delhi

If you purchased this book without a cover, you should be aware that this book is stolen property. It was reported as "unsold and destroyed" to the publisher, and neither the author nor the publisher has received any payment for this "stripped book."

SIMON & SCHUSTER BOOKS FOR YOUNG READERS
An imprint of Simon & Schuster Children's Publishing Division
1230 Avenue of the Americas, New York, New York 10020
This book is a work of fiction. Any references to historical events, real people, or real locales are used fictitiously. Other names, characters, places, and incidents are products of the author's imagination, and any resemblance to actual events or locales or persons, living or dead, is entirely coincidental.
Copyright © 2010 by Dan Gutman
All rights reserved, including the right of reproduction in whole or in part in any form.
SIMON & SCHUSTER BOOKS FOR YOUNG READERS is a trademark of
Simon & Schuster, Inc.
For information about special discounts for bulk purchases, please contact Simon & Schuster Special Sales at 1-866-506-1949 or business@simonandschuster.com.
The Simon & Schuster Speakers Bureau can bring authors to your live event. For more information or to book an event, contact the Simon & Schuster Speakers Bureau at 1-866-248-3049 or visit our website at www.simonspeakers.com.
Also available in a Simon & Schuster Books for Young Readers hardcover edition
Book design by Krista Vossen
The text for this book is set in Edlund.
Permission to use "Stacy's Mom"
Lyrics by Adam Schlesinger and Chris Collingwood
Copyright © 2003 Monkey Demon Music/Vaguely Familiar Music
Manufactured in the United States of America
0612 OFF
First Simon & Schuster Books for Young Readers paperback edition July 2012
2 4 6 8 10 9 7 5 3 1
The Library of Congress has cataloged the hardcover edition as follows:
Gutman, Dan.
The talent show / Dan Gutman.—1st ed.
p. cm.
Summary: After a devastating tornado destroys much of Cape Bluff, Kansas, residents come together as a community to put on a talent show as a fund-raiser.
ISBN 978-1-4169-9003-1 (hc)
[1. Talent shows—Fiction. 2. Tornadoes—Fiction. 3. Community life—Fiction.
4. Kansas—Fiction.] I. Title.
PZ7.G9846Tal 2010
[Fic]—dc22
2010005128
ISBN 978-1-4169-9004-8 (pbk)
ISBN 978-1-4391-5827-2 (eBook)

To all the folks at Simon & Schuster

Acknowledgments

· · · · · · · · · · · · · · · · · · ·

Thanks to Wendy and Jason Blau, Yonca and Jean Gerlach, Beth and Eric Levin, Meg Gallwitz, Mike Wilson, Kathleen Delaney, Nina Wallace, Donna Tambussi, and Caroll Stoner.

Part 1

Chapter 1

When the Tornado Hit . . .

- **Paul Crichton**, a fifth grader at Cape Bluff Elementary School in Cape Bluff, Kansas, was alone in his basement with his Fender Stratocaster guitar, trying to master the intro to "Stairway to Heaven."

- **Julia Maguire**, a Cape Bluff fourth grader, was on pointe at The Fontaneau Ballet Studio, rehearsing her relevés and tour jetés for the grand allegro in *Giselle*.

- **Elke Villa**, a sixth grader, was in the shower, belting out "I Will Survive," Gloria Gaynor's

1978 disco anthem, into a loofah that she was pretending was a microphone.

• **Richard Ackoon**, a third-grade aspiring rap star, was sitting on his back porch, paging through his rhyming dictionary, and trying to find a word that rhymed with "humiliate." He looked up and saw his father in the distance, working in the fields on his small farm.

• **Don Potash**, sixth grader, was listening through headphones while watching a stand-up comedy DVD, *Jerry Seinfeld: I'm Telling You for the Last Time.*

• **Lucille Rettino**, the fifty-five-year-old mayor of Cape Bluff, was being photographed with the members of the Cape Bluff Garden Club at their annual fund-raiser.

• **Jon Anderson**, the principal of Cape Bluff Elementary School, was at a desk in his office doing paperwork and sipping coffee.

- **Justin Chanda**, a multimillion-selling pop star who grew up in Cape Bluff, was a thousand miles away at a recording studio in Los Angeles, overdubbing vocals for his next album, *Back to Kansas*.

- **"Honest Dave" Gale** was on the lot of his car dealership, Honest Dave's Hummer Heaven, trying to talk a reluctant customer into buying a Hummer H3T pickup.

- **Mary Marotta**, a stay-at-home mom and proud member of the PTA, was watching *Oprah* while making peanut butter and Marshmallow Fluff sandwiches for her two young children, who had just come home from school.

But *everybody* in Cape Bluff, Kansas, stopped what they were doing when the tornado alarm sounded.

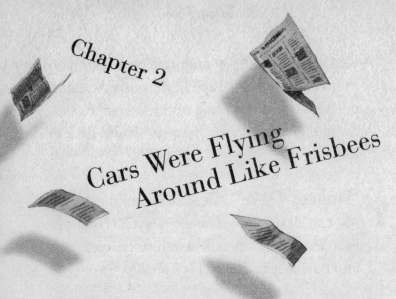

Chapter 2

Cars Were Flying Around Like Frisbees

The animals were the first to realize something was wrong. They always are. At 3:48 p.m. that Tuesday afternoon, the birds in Cape Bluff suddenly stopped singing. Cows huddled close together in the field. Dogs began running around erratically.

Animals have a sixth sense about these things. Maybe it's infrasound—low frequency rumbles that are below the threshold of human hearing.

Anyway, the animals knew before the people. They just knew.

To anyone's eyes in Cape Bluff, at first it looked like a whopper of a thunderstorm was approaching. The cumuliform clouds that dotted the sky all morning had, without anyone noticing, joined into one gigantic darker cloud mass covering the sky and blocking out the sun.

But there was something different this day. The sky took on a sickly yellow/greenish hue. At the local weather station a few miles down the road, a meteorologist jotted down the time in his logbook.

The rains came down for a while, not too heavy. There was even some hail. Then there was an eerie quiet.

Richard Ackoon, the young rapper sitting on his porch, looked up. There had been a sudden change in pressure. The air felt heavy, and hot, like it was too close to his face. He found it hard to breathe.

The enormous cloud was moving fast, and then, suddenly, the wind stopped. It was peaceful. The leaves in the trees tilted up gently, as if they were looking at the sky.

No funnel cloud was visible. Not yet. There was a subtle swirling mist, but nobody could see it. The tube of air was horizontal at first, but gradually the rising air pushed it vertically, until it resembled a spinning top.

Elke Villa, the girl who had been singing in the shower, suddenly stopped when she heard a tornado siren go off in the distance.

Cape Bluff is in the heart of Tornado Alley, a vast area that stretches from parts of Texas to Minnesota. Everyone who lives within that region knows what to do when the tornado siren blares. In school they had tornado drills once a month.

Elke quickly rinsed off and got out of the shower. She threw on a T-shirt and shorts, went into her bedroom, and pulled the mattress off her bed. Then she dragged it into the bathroom. She picked up her dog, Lucky, climbed into the tub, and pulled the mattress over the two of them. She and Lucky would stay there in the bathtub until the all-clear signal sounded.

Mrs. Mary Marotta quickly screwed the cap on the Marshmallow Fluff jar and grabbed the remote control to her TV. She flipped away from *Oprah* and turned to The Weather Channel. The screen was flashing TORNADO WARNING FOR FOUR STATE AREA. But almost instantly the power in her house went out and the screen faded to black. She rushed to get a flashlight and transistor radio from her pantry.

"Mommy, the TV went off!" cried her daughter, Elsie, from the living room. Elsie was in second grade, and her little brother, Edward, was in first.

Mrs. Marotta grabbed each of them by the arm, and hustled them outside to the prefab bomb shelter constructed belowground in the backyard. It had been built in the 1950s, in case of a Russian atomic blast.

When he heard the siren, Paul Crichton, the young guitar god, grabbed his most precious possession—his Strat—and crawled under the workbench in the corner of the basement. That's what his parents had taught him to do. If anything was going to fall on him—like the entire house—he would be protected.

At The Fontaneau Ballet Studio, Julia Maguire and the other students were hustled away from all that glass—the picture window in the front and the giant mirror that covered one whole wall of the studio. The school had no basement. The students were led—in an orderly fashion—into the office and instructed to crouch down in the corner to make as small a target as possible. The leotard-clad girls covered their heads with notebooks, backpacks, or in some cases, just their hands.

All over Cape Bluff, people rushed to prepare for a disaster. Some were hiding in closets, hoping to put as many walls as they could between themselves and the wind. People huddled on the floors of interior rooms, avoiding halls that opened to the outside in any direction. Kids rushed to put on their bike helmets, batting helmets, and hockey masks. Anything to protect themselves from flying objects. Some people crawled into metal trash cans. Parents were exchanging final glances, just in case they would not see one another again.

The storm picked up momentum as it rushed through town. People who were unfortunate enough to be out on the streets of Cape Bluff watched the black funnel approaching, fully aware that a falling tree, power line, or lightning bolt was just as dangerous as the tornado itself.

The smart ones jumped in a nearby ditch and lay there. That's the safest place outdoors, unless of course, you get swept away by a flash flood.

All over town, a continuous rumble could be heard in the distance. As the funnel moved closer, it became a muffled *whoosh*ing sound, like a waterfall or air rushing past an open car window driven at high speed. The roar grew sharper and louder, until it sounded like a freight train or jet engine.

It was officially an F4 tornado. The wind speed topped out at 260 miles per hour. But nobody knew the speed for sure, because at the weather station the device they used to measure wind speed blew away. Trees began to bend, and finally snap.

Some people—some foolish people—ran around their houses frantically opening the windows. They had been told that if the windows are open, it allows a tornado to pass through more easily and cause less destruction.

They were wrong.

The black funnel, now visible for miles, began to stab the earth like a dagger from the clouds. The snakelike tail flipped back and forth underneath it, licking one neighborhood for a minute or two before dancing on to the next one, like a bee trying to decide which flower to pollinate. It lashed out as if it had a purpose, an insatiable twisted mind intent on destroying anything below.

Like a carousel out of control, debris was swirling overhead. Bricks, beams, concrete, chairs, tables, clothes, toys, jewelry, and family heirlooms. Kitchen knives were flung 150 feet per second, impaling anything in their path. Years later, one would be found at a construction site, eight feet below the ground.

At Pete's Lumber Company on the north side of town, two-by-fours were being tossed around like Popsicle sticks. A hundred-year-old oak tree was yanked out by the roots. Cars were flying through the air like Frisbees.

At Cape Bluff Elementary School, the door to the library was ripped off its hinges. Water flooded inside, and virtually every book in the library was ruined.

At Booker's Stamps and Coins, the entire inventory was swept away. In an instant, a lifetime of work that had been so carefully collected and stored was gone.

Objects were plucked off the ground and thrown every which way. A pair of German shepherds was picked up and carried a quarter mile from their home. Miraculously, neither was hurt. An entire maple tree would be found, intact, two miles from where it grew. Forty miles away, a phone bill from a Cape Bluff resident would be found on the street. Debris would be picked up as far as eighty miles away.

Don Potash, the young comedian, had been home alone, watching his portable battery-powered DVD player. He had headphones on and hadn't heard a thing. As he listened to Jerry Seinfeld tell jokes about doing laundry, Don's house began to shudder as if a giant was shaking it. The building vibrated as the roar grew steadily louder. Don was concentrating heavily as he copied down the jokes in his special notebook that was filled with his favorite comedy routines.

By the time Don realized anything was going on, the aluminum siding was being ripped away from the frame of his house like a banana peel. And then, the building literally *exploded* and flew away. Seconds later, you couldn't even tell that a house had ever been on that spot. It had been wiped clean.

All that was left was Don Potash, sitting where his house used to be, dazed and confused, with the headphones still on his head.

And then, after all that . . . nothing. The tornado had done the only thing it knew how to do—destroy things indiscriminately. It suddenly dissipated, exhausted, like a car that had run out of gas.

Just ten minutes after the tornado started, it was all over.

Chapter 3

A Crazy Idea

"I'm just about busted, George."

Honest Dave admitted it to an old friend as they trudged up the steps of Cape Bluff High School three days later. Even though the tornado caused just minor damage to Honest Dave's Hummer Heaven, business had been way off for more than a year. Few people in town had enough money to buy a new car, especially the big gas guzzlers at Hummer Heaven. And the only people from out of town who were coming to Cape Bluff were gawkers who wanted to see what it looked like after a tornado had just about flattened a town. The tornado had delivered a knockout blow.

Honest Dave wiped his muddy feet before

entering the auditorium. He wore a jacket and tie, like always. People treat you with respect when you wear a jacket and tie. Nobody wants to buy a car from a slob. That's what Dave always said. He was a salesman's salesman. There are three kinds of people in the world, according to Dave: old customers, new customers, and potential customers.

A large percentage of Cape Bluff citizens (population: 1,098) had gathered at the high school for the seven o'clock town meeting. The football field out back had been torn up pretty badly, but the tornado had mercifully left the school alone. The auditorium was half-filled by the time Honest Dave got there, and people were still streaming in.

The official estimate, according to *The Cape Bluff Tribune*, was $34 million worth of damage, 168 trees down, thirty-five houses destroyed beyond repair, thirteen stores damaged, and nine cars totaled. One of those cars hadn't even been *found* yet. There had been hundreds of injuries, including twenty-four broken bones, a punctured lung, and at least one concussion. Miraculously, there had been no deaths. People in this part of the country know what to do when there's a tornado.

A brief history of Cape Bluff, Kansas. If you don't like to read brief histories, that's okay. Skip the next couple of pages.

The town is located where the flat plains and rolling hills of Oklahoma, Arkansas, Missouri, and Kansas just about meet at the corners. It was founded in 1842 as an Indian trading post. A U.S. army officer, LaRue Bluff, surveyed the town, and the Reverend Harris G. Cape founded the first Methodist congregation in the area. When it came time to give the place a name, Reverend Cape and Captain Bluff agreed to flip a coin. Defying all odds, the coin landed on its edge, and the town was officially named Cape Bluff in 1859.

There were about a thousand residents by the time of the Civil War, but Cape Bluff didn't get on a map until the arrival of the Missouri Western Railroad in 1872. Around the same time, zinc and lead were discovered in the area. Southern and Eastern European immigrants poured into Cape Bluff, starting up a foundry, a furniture factory, woolen and grain mills, a plow works, and other businesses. Cape Bluff grew, and at the turn of the twentieth century, ten thousand people lived there. It was one of the first towns in Kansas to have electricity.

An interesting side note: in 1933, Bonnie and Clyde spent several weeks hiding out at Cape Bluff after pulling off a string of bank robberies across the Midwest.

After World War II, the price of lead and zinc plummeted, and the fortunes of Cape Bluff with it. Most of the mines closed down, and the population dropped by half.

Today, there isn't much evidence of Cape Bluff's glory days. You can still find a few badly marked open pit mines and shafts that occasionally cave in, creating sink holes big enough to swallow large animals and small cars. The main street—Main Street—is cluttered with a Burger King and a few other fast-food joints, gas stations, a supermarket, a movie theater that doesn't show movies anymore, and the faded signs of businesses that picked up and moved elsewhere many years ago.

The rich folks, with their summer homes and designer cars, live in Kansas City, Tulsa, or Little Rock, each about three hours away. Cape Bluff is working class. You have to be tough to live there. Resilient. The people have survived two World

Wars, one Depression, countless recessions, gas shortages, crop failures, not to mention the occasional "weather event." Four tornadoes touched down in the 1990s, ruining countless lives.

There were a lot of downcast faces as people filed into the high school auditorium that Friday night. Many were wearing ripped clothes and soiled shoes, or walked with a limp. Some people had lost everything they owned. Tornado insurance was a luxury not many people could afford.

There were few smiling faces, and no laughter. Old friends hugged one another, relieved to see that the other was still alive.

Some people came to ask questions, to get advice, to see neighbors, or just to vent their anger. Some came for a Friday night out. It was something to do, and it didn't cost anything.

Reverend John Mercun, the pastor of First Presbyterian Church, greeted everyone as they lumbered up the steps.

"Maybe God didn't intend for people to live here, Pastor," said Honest Dave.

"God protected us, Dave," Reverend John assured him. "Nobody died."

Usually, it was Mayor Rettino who ran the town meetings. But on this night, she sat quietly on the stage with the other local politicians. There were no prepared speeches. Nobody wanted to take ownership of a natural disaster. It was left to the chief of police, Officer Michael Selleck, to tell everyone to take a seat and call the meeting to order.

A microphone had been set up in the front of the auditorium. People began lining up to wait their turn to speak. First in line was Bill Potash, the father of Don, the young Seinfeld fan.

"I rebuilt my house three times," he said before the microphone produced some squealing feedback. "Now it's gone. There's nothin' left. My truck is wrecked. The insurance doesn't cover tornadoes. We're living with my sister's family. And we're lucky to have 'em. But why is it always us? How much am I supposed to take?"

There were murmurs of sympathy through the auditorium.

Bill Potash wasn't expecting anyone to have a satisfying answer for him. He just wanted to say it out loud. Tears in his eyes, he went back and sat down next to his wife and son.

Honest Dave was next in line.

"I may have to shut down Hummer Heaven," he announced. "Nobody's buyin' big cars anymore. How am I supposed to sell anything when everybody wants to go fifty miles on a gallon of gas, and all I can give them is sixteen? I didn't see this coming. I guessed wrong, and now people are laughing at me."

"Nobody's laughing at you, Dave," somebody called from the audience.

Mary Marotta, the PTA mom who was making sandwiches in her kitchen when the tornado hit, stepped up to the microphone.

"If folks like you move out, we lose our tax base," she said to Honest Dave. "Fewer businesses means we have fewer places to shop. People move away. Then the schools start shutting down because there aren't enough kids. Then families don't move here because the schools aren't good. And then we become a ghost town. Don't leave, Dave."

"That's right," somebody hollered.

The crowd was mainly adults, but some kids came with their parents: Paul Crichton, Julia Maguire, Richard Ackoon, Elke Villa, and Don Potash, to name a few. Mostly, they sat quietly and listened. None of them knew anything about tax bases, insurance, or any of that financial mumbo jumbo. They just knew their parents were hurting.

Don fantasized for a moment about getting up at the microphone and lightening the mood by telling a few Seinfeld jokes he had memorized. But he was shy about talking in front of people, and he was afraid it might be too soon after the tornado for humor. From studying comedy, he had learned that it took years before people could handle jokes about national tragedies, like assassinations and September 11.

The next person in line at the mic was a short man who had come with just one simple question he wanted to ask.

"I want to know what are we supposed to do *now*?"

He was looking in the direction of Mayor Rettino. He wasn't the only one.

Lucille Rettino avoided making eye contact with the man. She fidgeted in her seat, wondering why the worst tornado in Cape Bluff history had to happen on *her* watch. She was at the end of her first term as mayor, and she was the first female mayor in the town.

Born and raised in Cape Bluff, she knew everybody, and everybody liked her. Most people didn't even know if she was a Republican or a Democrat. It didn't matter. Mayor Rettino cared about everybody and seemed to be just about everywhere, cutting ribbons to open a new store, giving out trophies at the Little League banquet, and always stopping to say hello to people on the street. She was instantly recognizable because of her silver hair and red clothes. Always red. She thought that would make people remember her, and it did.

But on this night, Mayor Rettino didn't want people to look at her. She was out of ideas anyway. How do you get people to cheer up when they know there will always be another tornado, another recession, another company that decides to move its factory to China?

Paul Crichton, the young guitarist who had been playing "Stairway to Heaven" in his basement when the tornado hit, stood up. He was a good-looking, confident boy and, unlike most kids, he had no problem with standing up to speak in front of a bunch of grown-ups. Paul made his way down to the front of the auditorium and got in line. After a few more grown-ups had their say, it was his turn.

"My name is Paul," he said, clearing his throat. "I'm a fifth grader at Cape Bluff Elementary School. We're studying American history right now, and if I learned one thing, it's that when we get knocked down, we get up again. Chicago was burned down by a fire in 1871. San Francisco was destroyed by an earthquake in 1906. Both towns were rebuilt and they became great American cities. Shouldn't it be the same here? We'll rebuild. That's what we do. Neighbors help neighbors. We all hang together, or we all hang separately. That's what Benjamin Franklin said. That's the American way, right?"

"You tell 'em, Paul!" somebody shouted from the back.

There was polite applause and a few "yeah"s as Paul went back to his seat. But there was no great enthusiasm. It wasn't like in the movies, when the coach gives the stirring halftime pep talk and the team charges out of the locker room all pumped up.

An old man took the microphone.

"You got good intentions, and I like that," he

said to Paul. "But you're a kid. I've lived in this town for more than fifty years, and I've seen it all. It's easy to say let's rebuild. Let's start over. That's fine for *you*. You've got your whole life ahead of you. But I don't want to start over. I'm *tired* of starting over every few years. It's not like I got some magic fairy dust I can sprinkle around and make my barn come back. These things cost money."

His confidence gone, Paul shrank down in his seat and tried to look small. His mother put an arm around him and whispered that it took a lot of courage to get up and say what he did in front of so many people. She was proud of him.

Nobody else was in line at the microphone. There was an awkward silence.

"May I say a few words?"

Everybody swiveled in their seats to see where the booming voice came from. Jon Anderson, the principal of Cape Bluff Elementary School, stood up. He didn't need a microphone.

Mr. Anderson didn't look like a principal. Barely thirty years old, he had been a fifth-grade teacher for eight years in Pennsylvania, and then went to graduate school in Oklahoma to get a master's degree. When the Cape Bluff principal died suddenly a year earlier, Anderson applied for the job and was surprised to get it.

"Go for it, Jon," somebody shouted.

"I'm new around here, as you know," Principal Anderson said. "I haven't lived through what you folks have experienced. I mean no disrespect, and I don't have a solution to your problems. I don't even know that there *is* a solution. But I just had a crazy idea."

"*This* I gotta hear," somebody muttered.

"Why don't we put on a talent show?" Principal Anderson said.

For the first time, smiles appeared on faces. There was some laughter, too, and heads shaking in disbelief. A buzz of muffled conversation filled the room.

"What?!"

"Did he just say we should put on *a talent show*?"

". . . you kidding me?"

". . . lost his marbles."

"I'm serious," Principal Anderson said.

One of the older residents, a farmer, stood up. "This is no time to be putting on a show," he said. "This town is flat on its back. Have some sense, boy."

A few heads nodded in agreement.

"Actually," Principal Anderson said, turning to face the old man, "I think this is the *ideal* time to put on a show. Paul is right. This town will rebuild, because that's what people do. But I propose that we do something *more*. I think we need something to take our minds off what happened to us. We need something to give this town a lift. Get us *excited* about something. Have a little *fun*. They had a yearly talent show at my old school, and it was always a huge success."

Principal Anderson sat back down. His wife patted him on the back. The auditorium was filled with muted discussions.

"I think a talent show is a *great* idea," said Julia Maguire, the fourth grader who had been stuck at her ballet school when the tornado hit.

"It could be like *American Idol!*" said Richard Ackoon, the young rapper.

The energy level in the room kicked up a notch. People started shouting out ideas without bothering to line up at the microphone.

"We can give a prize to the winner. . . ."

"We can use it as a fund-raiser to help repair the school library."

"How are ya gonna make money on a talent show?"

"We'll sell tickets."

". . . shoot a video and sell it."

". . . put it on YouTube . . ."

". . . sell refreshments."

"I'll bake a cake."

". . . print a program and sell ads in it."

Mayor Rettino had been silent up until this time. She liked what she was seeing—people getting involved. The spark of enthusiasm. She could ride that. Finally she stood up and went over to the microphone.

"It's an interesting idea, Mr. Anderson," she said, "but what are the costs? Have you thought about the budget to put on a show? If you give away a decent prize to the winner, that costs money. If you want to do a show right, you're going to want to have professional quality sound and lighting. That would set us back around three thousand dollars right there. Then you've got to print programs, and tickets. It all costs money."

Principal Anderson nodded his head. He

hadn't really thought the idea through.

A man in the back of the room stood up.

"Mayor," he said, "My name is Laurent Linn. I own Infinity Sound & Lighting Company on Montague Street. I just wanted to say that if you folks put on a talent show, I'll donate my equipment and services for the night. I want to see Cape Bluff get back on its feet, like everybody else."

Mr. Linn got a nice round of applause, and took a bow.

"Heck," he added. "I don't have any business anyway, since the tornado."

Honest Dave stood up. Nobody was going to out-donate *him*.

"Tell you what I'm gonna do, Mayor," he said. "For the grand prize, Honest Dave's Hummer Heaven is gonna donate a brand spanking new Hummer!"

"*Ooooooooooooooooh!*"

"How do you like *them* apples?" Honest Dave added.

"Uh, I hate to break it to you, Dave," Mayor Rettino said, "but children are not legally allowed to drive. What good is a car to a kid?"

"Hey, I sell cars," Honest Dave said, throwing

his hands in the air. "That's what I do. Give me a break. If you don't want the Hummer—"

"We'll take the Hummer!" Principal Anderson shouted quickly. "We'll take the Hummer!"

After that, some other local businesspeople jumped up. The owner of CopyCat Copy Shop offered to print the programs and tickets for free. A local photographer said she would shoot and edit a video of the show. Several moms volunteered to bake brownies, cookies, and cupcakes to be sold in the lobby. Just about every cost could be covered by somebody willing to make a donation. There was a sense of excitement in the auditorium.

Chief of Police Selleck felt the crowd was getting a little out of hand. He went to the front and took the microphone.

"Excuse me," he said, commanding the room's attention instantly. "There's just one problem with this idea of putting on a talent show. No offense, but where are you gonna get the *talent*? You can't have a talent show without talent."

There was a murmur of conversation, and Officer Selleck continued.

"I mean, let's face it, folks, this town hasn't had any *real* talent since Justin Chanda left."

Everyone in Cape Bluff knew about Justin Chanda, even if they never met him. A local kid, he started a teeny-bopper boy band named Pendulum Dune while he was still in high school. The group played its first gig right in the auditorium where they were sitting. After their debut album sold ten million copies, Justin left the group and became a hugely successful solo rhythm and blues artist. He hadn't been back to Cape Bluff since high school. That was ten years ago. He moved his parents to Los Angeles so they would be closer.

Principal Anderson stood up again.

"I beg to differ, Chief Selleck," he said. "I know of at least *one* young lady at Cape Bluff Elementary School who's got a voice like an angel. Her name is Elke Villa. I've heard her sing. She's remarkable."

Principal Anderson didn't realize that Elke was sitting right there, in the fourteenth row, next to her mother. Mrs. Villa beamed. Elke, who had been singing in the shower when the tornado hit, tried to be invisible. She knew she had a good voice. She could tell because whenever she opened her mouth to sing, people would stop what they were doing and stare at her with angelic looks on their faces. She kind of liked the attention, and at the same time, it was a little embarrassing. Her face flushed red. Elke wasn't even sure if she would enter a school talent show.

"So we put on a talent show for just one kid?" Officer Selleck asked, as if Elke wasn't sitting there. "We might as well just hand her the keys to that Hummer right now."

"That's right!" somebody agreed.

Paul Crichton, his confidence surging again, hustled down the aisle to grab the microphone.

"If you ask me, this town has *plenty* of talent," he said. "Nothing against Elke, but I think my band The BluffTones would give her a run for the money in a talent show."

"*Ooooooh!*" rumbled the crowd. Everybody loves a challenge.

Elke turned around in her seat to look at Paul. He was one grade below her at school. They had talked a few times, but barely knew each other. She didn't like the idea of a younger kid suggesting he was better than her.

"There are a lot of other talented kids in this town too," Paul said. "And by the way, I'm twelve, and that Hummer can sit in our driveway for four years until I'm old enough to drive it. No problem."

Mayor Rettino banged the gavel a few times to restore order in the auditorium.

"Before we decide any course of action," she said, "does anybody have any *other* ideas they would like to propose at this time?"

Silence. And then a man wearing a cowboy hat stood up.

"How about we turn Cape Bluff into a sorta living tornado museum?" he suggested. "We can charge folks to come in and see the damage. Like, five bucks a head."

More silence. You could almost hear crickets chirping.

"So," Mayor Rettino said, "if I understand you correctly, sir, you suggest that instead of rebuilding Cape Bluff, we just live amongst the rubble indefinitely so people can *look* at it?"

"Yeah, somethin' like that," the man said. "Tourists are comin' here now to see the devastation, right? Over the long term, we make money off 'em. And it'll be educational, too. Folks will learn about the destructive force of nature."

"With all due respect, sir," Officer Selleck said,

"that's just about the dumbest idea I ever heard."

"I say we put it to a vote!" shouted Honest Dave Gale.

"I second that," said Bill Potash.

Slips of paper were passed across the auditorium from row to row. People fumbled in their pockets and purses looking for pens and pencils.

"Mark down a *T* if you think we should put on a talent show," Police Chief Selleck announced, "and mark down an *R* if you want to charge people to come look at our rubble."

It took about twenty minutes to gather up all the slips of paper and tally the results. Mayor Rettino stepped up to the microphone to make the announcement.

"Okay, we have six hundred and seventy-nine votes for a talent show," she said, "and one hundred twenty-one votes for a rubble museum."

The audience erupted in applause and cheering.

"Well," said Officer Selleck, "it looks like we're putting on a show."

Part 2

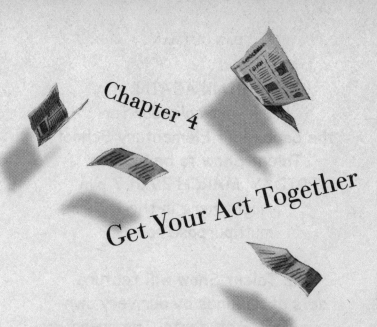

Chapter 4

Get Your Act Together

"People try to put us d-d-d-d-down . . ."

Paul Crichton came charging two steps at a time up to the front entrance of Cape Bluff Elementary School the next Monday morning. He had his iPod turned up *way* too loud. But when you're listening to "My Generation" by The Who, you *have* to play it full blast.

Before he yanked open the door, Paul saw this flyer taped to it . . .

GET READY TO BOOGIE!!!
Do you think you've got talent?
PROVE IT!
Think you don't?

THINK AGAIN!
Mark your calendar for
the Cape Bluff Elementary School
Talent Show to be held on
FRIDAY, MARCH 29 at 7 p.m.
right here in the
multipurpose room.

The Talent Show will feature
acts of all kinds by our very own
grade 3–6 students. The grand
prize is a brand-new Hummer H3T
pickup (thanks to Honest Dave's
Hummer Heaven). The theme of
the talent show is "The Beach,"
but you do not HAVE to perform
to the theme.

Auditions will be held this Friday
after school in the multipurpose
room. Be there or be square! GET
YOUR ACT TOGETHER! We will
also need people to work on the
stage crew.

Paul pumped his fist and made a mental note to call a band meeting after school.

Inside, Mrs. Mary Marotta was rushing around, trying to tape the same flyer up all over the hallways before they were filled with students. She assigned her own kids, second grader Elsie and first grader Edward, to tear off pieces of tape and hand them to her.

After the town had voted to hold a talent show, Principal Anderson realized he was far too busy to run it himself. His teachers were swamped with work. What he needed was an enthusiastic parent volunteer. Cape Bluff is a small town. Everybody knows everybody. He asked around for someone who had theatrical experience, and the name Mary Marotta kept coming up.

Mrs. Marotta, ten years earlier, had been quite an actress. She was in the high school play every year, and won the lead roles in *My Fair Lady* and *Grease*. She was Miss Cape Bluff in the 4th of July parade. After graduation, her friends urged her to move to New York City and become a star on Broadway. Instead, she moved down the street from her parents, married the quarterback of the high school football team, and started a family.

The marriage didn't last, unfortunately. It was her husband that ended up moving to New York, to become a stockbroker. Mary didn't regret the decision she made, but always wondered how her life would have been different if she had chased her dream.

Running the talent show would be a big job. She wasn't sure she could handle it, with Elsie and Edward tagging along everywhere. But once she agreed to do it, Mrs. Marotta threw herself into the talent show headfirst. That's the kind of person she was.

After the flyers were all taped up on the walls, Mary drove home, sat at her computer, and typed up a second page to the flyer, which would be put into everyone's backpacks at the end of the day. . . .

TALENT SHOW DETAILS . . .

- All acts must be two minutes or shorter.
- We encourage children to perform as <u>groups</u>. That way, more students will be able to participate.

- All acts that are using a CD for background music must bring it to their audition.
- Start thinking about costumes and props NOW.
- We will have mandatory technical and dress rehearsals.
- All acts, songs, and costumes must be appropriate for a family audience. There will be no violence, no guns, and NO NINJAS.
- If you are performing a song, bring the title and a hard copy of the lyrics with you to your audition. We want to make sure two groups don't perform the same song.
- The judges of the talent show will be Cape Bluff Mayor Lucille Rettino, Principal Jon Anderson, and Reverend John Mercun of the First Presbyterian Church. They do not accept donations, cash, or other bribes!

In the hallways and in the lunchroom, the talent show was the big topic of conversation among the students. There were a lot of whispers at the lockers: "Do you want to be in a group with me?" "Are you joining a group with *her*?" "Do you think she would join our group?" "What song should we sing?"

From the start, some kids knew exactly what they would perform, down to the song title and dance steps. Others knew they wanted to be in the show, but weren't sure if they had enough talent—and courage—to get up on a stage with lots of people looking at them. Still others—almost all boys— wanted no part. They joked among themselves, and said the whole idea of a talent show was stupid.

Just before school let out for the day, Honest Dave Gale carefully drove a candy-apple red Hummer H3T pickup over the curb and parked it on the grass right in front of the Cape Bluff Elementary School sign.

He got out and put this sign on the windshield:

SHOW YOUR TALENT
THIS TRUCK COULD BE YOURS
COURTESY OF
HONEST DAVE'S HUMMER HEAVEN

When the three o'clock bell rang, the front doors opened, and in seconds kids were pouring out of the school.

As he walked by the Hummer on the lawn, Paul Crichton thought about which song his band would perform in the talent show. Two minutes was not a lot of time. Something peppy, he figured. Something familiar that would get the crowd clapping and singing along. A classic song that parents and kids would like. And something that *rocked*.

As she walked by the Hummer, Elke Villa made up her mind and decided that she would enter the talent show, and sing by herself. Now the only question was, should she go with a new hit song that was on the radio and all the kids knew, or maybe a timeless standard that would appeal more to the judges and grown-ups in the audience?

As he walked by the Hummer, Richard Ackoon was already mixing and matching words and rhymes in his head, composing a rap that would blow away even the people in the audience who hated rap music. Maybe something about the tornado.

As she walked by the Hummer, Julia Maguire sighed. She would have liked to dance in the talent show. But there was no way she was going to get up in front of all those people and do ballet by herself. The kids would laugh her off the stage.

As he walked by the Hummer, Don Potash thought about his dad's truck, which was now lying sideways in a ditch a hundred feet from where his house used to be. He thought about how much it would mean to his dad if he could win the Hummer H3T pickup. The only problem was that he had no talent and had never even been on a stage before.

Just about every student in the school walked by the Hummer and thought about what he or she could do in the talent show.

Chapter 5

Elke Villa

If they held a "Most Likely to Succeed" survey at Cape Bluff Elementary School, there's no doubt that Elke Villa would be the winner.

When Elke walked into a room, it seemed to brighten. The chemistry changed. All eyes turned to her. She didn't try to make that happen. She didn't *have* to try.

It wasn't just her looks. Oh, she was pretty, with long, brown, impossibly straight hair. But a lot of girls are pretty. She had a great voice, too. People compared it to Beyoncé's. But lots of pretty girls have great voices. And it wasn't her unusual Swedish name. Elke had something special—that mysterious quality they call charisma.

It had always been that way. When she was three, Elke got up at her birthday party and sang a version of "New York, New York" that people still talk about. Grown-ups stopped eating their cake and ice cream in mid-bite. Nobody had ever heard a girl so young sing so well, so confidently.

Her father, Tom Villa, was a construction worker of distant Cherokee/Mexican descent who came to Kansas from Mississippi for the work. He married a Swedish girl who was born and raised in Cape Bluff. Mrs. Villa worked for a few years as a receptionist after high school, but gave it up after Elke and her two little brothers were born.

The Villas were one of the poorer families in Cape Bluff. Tom's job wasn't full-time, and when there was no construction work to be done, food stamps were required to put a decent dinner on the table. Elke didn't realize she was poor until sixth grade, when she started noticing that other kids had bigger houses, newer clothes, and more stuff than she did.

"Can we get a piano, Mom?" she asked one night after dinner.

"With your voice, we don't need a piano," her

mother replied. "One day you'll be able to hire a *dozen* piano players."

It was Elke's mom, Ingrid, who recognized her daughter's potential early and saw it as their ticket out of poverty. She did odd jobs—babysitting, pet sitting, house cleaning—and used the money she earned to pay for Elke's singing lessons. Mrs. Villa took Elke for private speech therapy to help her lose her hardly noticeable lisp.

The Villas couldn't afford acting lessons, so as soon as Elke knew how to read, her mother borrowed scripts of plays from the library. At night, instead of bedtime stories, the two of them would read lines from Shakespeare. Just about everything her mother did revolved around making Elke famous.

Elke was barely five when Mrs. Villa took her to a talent agency several hours away in Oklahoma City. Test photos were taken, and a few weeks later Elke was modeling snowsuits in a department store's advertising circular that was in the Sunday *Cape Bluff Tribune*.

"See? You're getting famous already!" Ingrid Villa told Elke the day the paper came out. She bought ten copies.

Mrs. Villa brought those photos of Elke on countless auditions for TV commercials advertising everything from shampoo to sofa beds. Elke almost got a part in a Duncan Hines commercial, but she didn't smile enough while she was eating chocolate cake, and the talent agency chose another girl. Eventually, the modeling jobs dried up and Mrs. Villa's old Ford Escort kept breaking down on the weekly drive to Oklahoma City. Elke was thrilled. She hated going to auditions and having to pose and smile for pictures.

Mrs. Villa began dragging Elke to outdoor festivals, country fairs, malls, open mic nights, and karaoke contests around Cape Bluff when she was in fourth grade. None of them paid much for singers, but when she opened her mouth, people noticed. Elke's name was getting around. There was always the chance that somebody with influence might spot her talent and take her to the next level. That was always what it was about, Mrs. Villa reminded her, getting to the next level.

"Can I go play now?" Elke was always asking.

"After you finish your vocal chord exercises," her mother insisted.

Elke's father had little confidence that show business would lead anywhere. He worked with his hands. It was hard for him to understand that anyone could make a living by singing, acting, or posing for pictures. When Elke went to bed at night, her parents would argue about it. They fought a lot. There was a lot of yelling and crying. Mr. Villa thought his wife should get a job and help support the family. She said she already *had* a full-time job—managing Elke's career. In fact, some days she would be up past midnight sending out head shots, burning CDs, and blasting out e-mails to Oprah, Ellen, Jay Leno, the *Today* show, *American Idol*, and anyone she could think of who might give Elke her big break. Nobody ever wrote back, but Mrs. Villa was convinced it was just a matter of time. If you keep trying, everyone always said, you will break through.

In the beginning, she personally chose Elke's repertoire. She would sing the standards— "Autumn Leaves," "Baby, It's Cold Outside," "Stardust," "What A Wonderful World," and familiar Broadway show tunes. But by fifth grade, Elke was starting to rebel.

"I don't want to be the next Barbra Streisand!"

she would yell. "I don't like Liza Minnelli! That's old-time music!"

"What do you want to be?" her mother asked. "Some hillbilly?"

"Yes!"

Elke wanted to be the next Patsy Cline or Dolly Parton. The music she listened to was country—Shania Twain, LeAnn Rimes, and the Dixie Chicks. These were her heroes.

After a few shouting matches, Mrs. Villa realized she couldn't force the great American songbook down Elke's throat. She also realized she could have the next Taylor Swift on her hands if she played her cards right. In fact, Mrs. Villa thought about moving the family to Los Angeles or Nashville, home of the country music business. But her husband refused to move.

As Elke was getting known around Cape Bluff, people began to gossip that Mrs. Villa was an overbearing stage mom who lived vicariously through Elke. And if you don't know what that means, it's a lot like those dads who push their sons to be sports heroes because they struck out with the bases loaded when *they* were twelve.

But the truth was that nobody was twisting

Elke's arm. She loved to sing, she wanted to become a singer when she grew up, and she had a competitive streak in her. Elke had grown up watching an endless parade of teenage girls—Hilary Duff, Miley Cyrus, Lindsay Lohan, Miranda Cosgrove—come out of nowheresville and become superstars. Every year, it seemed, some new fresh face would appear on Nick or Disney and become the next big thing. There must be a constant need to supply the world with young female pop stars. Everybody was always telling her that her voice was much better than any of those teenybopper girls.

To most people in Cape Bluff, it was inevitable that Elke would become a superstar one day. The only reason she hadn't hit it big already was because her parents didn't have the money to get her to the next level. Acting lessons, voice coaches, fancy wardrobes, and hair stylists are expensive. It's hard to get noticed in Cape Bluff, Kansas. You've got to go to Hollywood.

When the talent show was announced, Mrs. Villa thought it could be Elke's springboard to the next level. There would be local media there. The video would be on YouTube. It could go viral. You never know. This was how careers got launched.

The word around Cape Bluff was that Elke Villa winning the talent show was just about a done deal. It was in the bag. Some people even felt they shouldn't bother having the show at all. They might as well just give the Hummer to Elke and get it over with. The rumor was that if she won, her mom was planning to get a divorce and drive Elke to the West Coast or Nashville to take a shot at the big time.

There was just one problem.

Elke Villa was not even going to be *in* the talent show.

Chapter 6

Paul Crichton

While Elke was a reluctant celebrity with a lot of talent, Paul Crichton had very little talent but wanted to be famous *very* badly.

He wasn't at all musical, at least not when he was little. His dad had a huge CD collection that played constantly in his car and every room of the house, so Paul couldn't help but absorb some of his dad's love of 1970s rock and roll. But for his first ten years, he had no interest in music at all.

In second grade, it was a requirement that every student at Cape Bluff Elementary take up a musical instrument. There was an assembly in which the music teacher demonstrated the violin, snare drum, trumpet, cello, and several other instruments. Then the students got to pick the one they wanted to learn, and they rented that instrument from the school.

Paul chose the flute. He didn't particularly like the sound of the flute, or the way it looked. Paul chose the flute for one reason—it would be easy to carry to and from school. Who wanted to lug a French horn on the bus every day?

In the end, he didn't have a clue about how to read music or play the flute. Blowing air over the thing while moving his fingers to push down the pads over those little holes was confusing. It didn't come naturally. Paul spent more time polishing the flute than he did practicing with it. The day the students no longer had to take music lessons, Paul was first in line to return the flute to the music room.

He ignored music and turned to skateboarding through third and fourth grades, deciding that he wanted to become a famous skater when he grew up.

"After I win a gold medal in the X-Games," he told his friends confidently, "every company in the world will want me to endorse their products. I'll make *millions*."

Unfortunately, Paul soon discovered that in order to get really good at skateboarding, you have to be at least a little crazy. You need to take risks and fall down a lot trying to perfect your tricks. The best skaters tend to get hurt a lot. They bleed. They break bones.

Falling down, bleeding, and breaking bones were interesting to watch on video, but not things Paul wanted to experience personally. That stuff *hurts*! So much for a career as a pro skater. He toyed briefly with the idea of being a famous skateboard designer, but lacking any artistic ability, Paul gradually admitted to himself that maybe skateboarding would not be his ticket to fame and fortune.

Then one day, he was on vacation in Oregon visiting his cousin, who had an electric guitar lying around his bedroom. A song came on the radio—"Seven Nation Army" by a group called The White Stripes.

It consisted mainly of seven notes.

Duh . . . duh-duh-duh . . . duh-duh . . . duh

Duh . . . duh-duh-duh . . . duh-duh . . . duh

"Cool tune," he told his cousin.

It was a simple, catchy melody, and it repeated

over and over again. Paul picked up his cousin's guitar. He plucked the A string, the second one from the top, and slid his finger up the neck until the sound matched the first note of "Seven Nation Army." It was the seventh fret. The second note was the same, so he plucked it again. Then he slid his finger up to the tenth fret, where he found the third note. Then back down to the seventh fret. Then he slid his finger down to the fifth, third, and second frets. Before the song was over on the radio, he had figured out the seven-note musical phrase.

Duh . . . duh-duh-duh . . . duh-duh . . . duh

At the time, he didn't even know what notes he was playing—E . . . E-G-E . . . D-C . . . B. He just knew they sounded right.

Paul played the phrase over and over again until it sounded just like The White Stripes. The rest of the family was impressed that he could pick the song up so quickly, and Paul felt good when they complimented him. In the next few days, he played "Seven Nation Army" so many times, everybody started telling him to knock it off.

"Can't you play something *else* for a change?" his aunt begged.

During that week, something clicked in Paul's head. Rock and roll had grabbed him. When he got home, he put his skateboard down in the basement for good and made an announcement at the dinner table.

"I decided that I'm going to become a rock star when I grow up."

He raided his piggy bank and bought a used Fender Stratocaster and a cheap amplifier from a high school kid down the street who was happy to get rid of them.

Paul's parents wanted to encourage his new interest, which was certainly a lot safer than grinding rails and attempting kickflips off the church steps. But there was no money in the Crichton budget for guitar lessons.

So Paul went to the library and found a sheet music book that had guitar chord diagrams. On each page, above the musical notation, there were pictures of chords, like this:

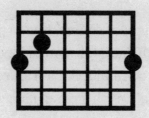

After a bit of fumbling, Paul figured out that the vertical lines represented the six strings on the guitar, the horizontal lines were the frets on the neck, and the black dots indicated where you put your fingers. He strummed his first chord.

And as it says in the Bible—it was good.

Paul quickly learned the major chords, the minor chords, and the seventh chords. Now he could play songs.

He began to listen to music, almost obsessively. The pop stars that most of the other kids at school idolized didn't grab him. He didn't like rap, hip-hop, or techno music created by machines. The boy bands and teenybopper girls who were on Radio Disney all the time just sounded silly to him. The music that really got his juices flowing was the "old time rock and roll" his dad had been pumping into his ears since he was a baby. The Beatles. The Stones. The Who. Led Zep. AC/DC. Clapton. Page. Hendrix. The ancient guitar gods of yesteryear.

The next step, of course, was to put together a band. A *killer* band. Not many kids in Cape Bluff were into old rock and roll. Paul asked around, and finally found a fourth grader named Jim Conlin who could play bass guitar a little. A guy named Victor Iannone was drumming on the table at lunch, and it turned out he had a full drum set at home—bass, snare, tom-toms, cymbals. The works. Paul asked him to join his band. Hanging around the music store at the mall, Paul found a sixth grader named Rob Goodman who could play the lead guitar part to "Free Bird" without even looking at his fingers. That was the *only* song he could play, but at least he could play *something*. With a little gentle persuasion, Rob joined the band too.

A practice was scheduled over at Victor's house, because the drum set was in his garage and it was a big hassle to set it up and take it down all the time. Paul could tell after a few minutes of jamming that the other guys weren't very good. But you don't have to be that good to play basic three-chord rock and roll. Just about anybody can play "Wipeout" without embarrassing themselves. Most importantly, the four boys had fun playing together as a band. None of them were into sports—unlike just about every other guy at school—but they all liked to play music. And being in a rock band—like being a skateboarder—was cool.

The band needed a name. The Fender Benders. Death By Squirrel. Ambidextrous Scissors Magnetic Bunions. After a night of throwing out a few hundred ridiculous ideas, they settled on The BluffTones.

None of the boys could sing particularly well, which can be a problem unless a band is just going to play "Wipeout" over and over again. But Paul knew there was one kid in the school who had a great voice.

Elke Villa.

Paul had heard Elke sing in chorus. Her voice just soared over everyone else's. With that voice and Paul's guitar, he imagined The BluffTones would go far. Maybe all the way to the top.

As founder and leader of the band, Paul took it upon himself to approach Elke. He was a little nervous. After all, she was a sixth grader and he was just in fifth. But he worked up the courage and walked over to her locker at the end of eighth period one day.

"Hi," he said. "You have a really great voice."

Elke looked at him. Was this little fifth grader asking her out on a *date* or something?

"Thanks," she mumbled, shutting her locker and turning to walk away.

"Listen," he said, stopping her. "Me and some guys formed a rock band, and we're pretty good. But we need a lead singer. And I was thinking—"

"I'm not really into rock," Elke said simply, "but thanks anyway."

She walked away and left him standing there. Paul wasn't mad. Disappointed, definitely. Well, maybe he was a *little* mad. Nobody wants to be rejected.

The great thing about rock and roll, Paul convinced himself, is that you can have a lousy voice and *still* be a star. Plenty of rock groups have lousy singers. Half of them just shout anyway. The heck with it. *He* would be the singer. The singer is the front man, the face of the band. Who needs Elke anyway? He didn't have to play second fiddle to some chick singer.

Once The BluffTones had learned how to play a dozen songs, they got their first gig—a birthday party for Victor Iannone's brother in third grade. It was at a bowling alley. The boys loaded up all their gear in Victor's mom's minivan, and felt like a real touring band. At the party, they ran through all the songs they knew, and the little kids jumped around, having a great time. Paul felt exhilarated performing in front of an audience, even if it was a bunch of little kids who didn't know The Beatles from Britney Spears.

At the end of the party, while the boys were packing up their equipment, Victor's mother came over and handed each of The BluffTones a twenty-dollar bill.

"Wow!" Paul exclaimed, "I didn't know we were getting paid for this!"

"If we hired a clown or magician," Mrs. Iannone told him, "it would have cost us a lot more. You guys are good. You could make some real money doing this."

That was all it took to get the wheels turning in Paul's head. He printed up a hundred business cards on his computer:

THE BLUFFTONES

"Today's music ain't got the same soul. I like that old-time rock and roll."

Music for parties, weddings, funerals, all occasions. We play good.

Call Paul Crichton: 555-9635

Paul's mother pointed out that "We play good" was not grammatically correct, and that people don't hire bands to play at funerals. But the cards were already printed, and he didn't want to make them over again.

Paul put a card up on every bulletin board he could find and waited for the phone to ring, but it never did. After the tornado hit Cape Bluff, nobody was looking to hire a rock band for *anything*. But as soon as the town decided to hold a talent show, Paul knew it would be great exposure for The BluffTones. Even if they didn't win, the whole town would see them in action. This could get the band a lot of gigs down the line. Maybe people would stop talking about Elke Villa and her great voice for a few minutes.

As Paul walked home from school that day, he thought about which song The BluffTones should play at the talent show. Maybe they should stick with something basic that all the guys in the band knew, like "Wild Thing," "Louie Louie," or "Satisfaction." Or maybe they should go with something more challenging, like "Stairway to Heaven." But if they messed up "Stairway," it would look really bad.

When he got home, he flipped on the radio in his room, like always. And this is what he heard:

Stacy, can I come over after school?
We can hang around by the pool
Did your mom get back from her business trip?
Is she there, or is she trying to give me the slip?

Whoa! What's *that*? It sounded like a classic rock song, but Paul had never heard it before. He turned up the volume.

You know, I'm not the little boy that I used to be
I'm all grown-up now, baby can't you see?

Stacy's mom has got it goin' on
She's all I want and I've waited for so long
Stacy, can't you see you're just not the girl for me
I know it might be wrong but I'm in love with Stacy's mom

It was irresistible! Totally catchy. Paul turned the volume higher and started dancing around his bedroom during the second verse.

Stacy, do you remember when I mowed your lawn?
Your mom came out with just a towel on
I could tell she liked me from the way she stared
And the way she said, "You missed a spot over there"
And I know that you think it's just a fantasy
But since your dad walked out, your mom could use a guy like me

Stacy's mom has got it goin' on
She's all I want and I've waited for so long
Stacy, can't you see you're just not the girl for me
I know it might be wrong but I'm in love with Stacy's mom

The song ended abruptly, and the DJ didn't identify it. Paul went to his computer to google the words "Stacy's Mom" and found that the song was a big hit in 2003 by a group called Fountains of Wayne. He then googled "Stacy's Mom chords" and found that the song was easy to play. It was almost all E, A, and B, with two tricky chords thrown in—G sharp minor and C sharp minor.

At the meeting that night, Paul gathered the band around his computer and showed them the YouTube video of "Stacy's Mom." Everyone loved it, and couldn't wait to start rehearsing. In an hour, they were able to play "Stacy's Mom" all the way through.

The BluffTones had found their song for the talent show.

Chapter 7

Julia Maguire

Julia started taking ballet lessons when she was four years old. She was walking down Main Street in Cape Bluff one day, holding hands with her mom, when they happened to pass by the big picture window of the Fontaneau Ballet Studio. Julia pressed her nose against the glass and saw a group of teenage girls in their leotards, jumping, pirouetting, and gliding on the tips of their toes. She was transfixed. Dancing was something she did at home all the time for fun, but it hadn't even occurred to her that you could go to a school and learn how to do it better.

"Can I come here, Mommy?" she pleaded.

Julia was two years too young to enroll in

Fontaneau. But because she seemed so intent on dancing, an exception was made, and Julia became the youngest student ever at the studio.

All the other girls in her class at school played soccer, but chasing a ball up and down a muddy field in the rain just seemed silly to Julia. She wanted to wear a beautiful costume and gracefully curve her body into an elegant arabesque. She started with an afternoon dance class once a week that first year, and liked it so much that she was eventually taking a class every day after school. By the time she got to fourth grade, just about all her time outside of school was devoted to dancing. She did her homework at night.

Julia wasn't a show-off. Just the opposite. While she loved to dance, she didn't like people staring at her while she did it. When it came time for her first ballet recital, her mother had to talk Julia into going. Her teacher asked her to do a short solo number, but she refused. Julia would only participate if she was up there on the stage with a bunch of other girls at the same time.

When the talent show was announced, she didn't want to audition for it. Only a few kids at school knew that she danced. She was afraid everybody would think ballet wasn't cool. The last thing she wanted was to get up in front of the whole school so everybody could laugh at her.

Her mother had other ideas. Mrs. Maguire was a "people person." She loved to be the center of attention and couldn't understand why Julia was so shy. The talent show seemed like the perfect opportunity for her daughter to finally come out of her shell. Once the students saw this other side of Julia, Mrs. Maguire argued, it would give her more confidence in social situations. She would make some friends. Mrs. Maguire had it all planned out in her mind.

"It would be a shame if you weren't in the talent show," she told Julia. "You're so talented. I was thinking that you should perform the wedding scene in *Sleeping Beauty*. You looked so lovely at your recital. Or maybe you should do the grand allegro in *Giselle*."

"I'll think it over" was as far as Julia would go.

The day after the talent show posters went up in the hallways, a girl named Anne Zafian walked over to Julia during gym class.

Anne was one of the "popular girls," as Julia called them. They were a small group of thin, pretty girls who had nicer clothes and lived in bigger houses with parents who drove newer cars than most of the people in Cape Bluff.

"I heard that you're a good dancer," Anne said.

"I'm okay," Julia replied.

"Well, a few of us are going to get together and do an act for the talent show," Anne said. "Do you want to be in it?"

Julia could hardly believe it. Anne Zafian had never spoken to her before. *None* of the popular girls had ever spoken to her before. Julia figured she wasn't cool enough to be part of their crowd, or her hair wasn't straight enough, or blond enough, or *something*.

"What kind of an act is it?" Julia asked.

"Oh, we'll do a dance and lip synch to a hip-hop song," Anne told her. "We need somebody who's good. Come on, it'll be fun."

"Can I think about it?"

"Think fast," Anne said. "I need an answer tomorrow, so we'll have time to ask somebody else before the auditions on Friday."

Julia thought it over during her ballet class that afternoon. There were some good reasons to join Anne's group.

First of all, it was flattering to have the most popular girl in fourth grade invite you to be a part of her act. If she was hanging around with the popular girls, she would be popular too. Second, if she joined Anne's group, she wouldn't have to be up on stage all by herself. There was safety in numbers. If she made a mistake, people might not even see it. Finally, Principal Anderson had encouraged everybody to put together group acts so more kids would be able to participate in the talent show.

When her mom came to pick her up at the end of ballet class, Julia broke the news to her. She had decided to be in a hip-hop lip synch act with Anne and the popular girls.

Mrs. Maguire had mixed feelings about the whole thing. She was happy that Julia had been invited to join a group, but disappointed that she wouldn't be able to show off her real talent.

"Hip-hop?" she said. "You've never danced hip-hop. And lip-synching? Julia, that's not even a *talent*. That's just moving your mouth while somebody with real talent sings."

"I want to be with my friends," Julia said.

"Friends?" Mrs. Maguire snorted. "Did any of

those girls ever come over to our house? Did any of them ever invite you to *their* house?"

"They're inviting me *now*," Julia said. "They want me to be their friend *now*. You wouldn't understand."

The old "you wouldn't understand" line. It defeats any argument.

"Do these so-called friends even *know* how to dance?" asked Mrs. Maguire.

"I don't know," Julia told her mother, "and I don't care."

"It's your life," Mrs. Maguire said, shaking her head. She couldn't stop thinking of the hundreds of hours Julia had spent practicing ballet, and the thousands of dollars spent on dance lessons. And now Julia wanted to prance around on stage lip-synching and dancing hip-hop with the popular girls. What a waste.

In the lunchroom the next day, Anne waved at Julia to come over. She brought her tray to the table where Anne was sitting with the other popular girls—Jessie, Chloe, Caroline, Jenny, and Katie.

"I thought it over, " Julia said. "I'll do it!"

All the girls slapped hands with her and welcomed her to the group. They agreed to get together at Anne's house that night for a rehearsal. Nobody mentioned the talent show for the rest of the lunch period. There was a lot of giggling and gossiping about kids at the other tables. Julia mostly listened. She was afraid she might say something stupid.

During lunch, Julia was a little ashamed of her peanut butter and jelly sandwich and her plain brown lunch bag. The other girls, she noticed, had fancy insulated bags with photos on them. They were all texting on their cell phones as they ate. Julia was the only one who didn't have a cell phone. Still, it was fun eating lunch at the popular table. *So this is what it's like to be at the top of the food chain,* she thought. She could get used to it.

That night, Julia's mother dropped her off at Anne's. It was one of the biggest houses in Cape Bluff. Mrs. Maguire kissed her and said she'd pick her up at nine o'clock. Julia had asked her mom to park around the corner, so nobody would see their old car. For a minute or so, Mrs. Maguire was mad. *What's* wrong *with this car? What's wrong with* me? Eventually, she was able to let it go, chalking it up to adolescent weirdness.

Anne's mom opened the front door to greet Julia. She looked like one of those "real housewives" you see on reality TV shows. She was dressed like she was going to a fancy dinner party. As they went inside, Julia noticed that the house was very neat. There wasn't stuff scattered all over the place, like in *her* house. It didn't look like people lived in this house.

Anne, Jessie, Chloe, Caroline, Jenny, and Katie were down the basement, in a room that was bigger than Julia's entire ballet school. Posters of popular boy bands covered the walls. The girls were giggling, gossiping, and eating chips and pretzels. Julia tried to act natural, but kept wondering when they would start rehearsing.

Finally, Anne's mother came downstairs. She said that she used to be a cheerleader, and had some ideas for a dance routine to show the girls.

"The theme of the talent show is 'The Beach,'" Mrs. Zafian said as she put a CD into a boom box on the floor. "So what do you think of this?"

Strange techno beach music started playing, and Anne's mom began dancing around the basement. She was *embarrassingly* bad. Julia looked around to see if any of the girls were giggling, but for once they weren't. In fact, they gave Mrs. Zafian a big round of applause when she was done.

She said she hired a local DJ to create a mix tape of electronic hip-hop beach music. She had also ordered matching bathing suits for the girls to wear at the talent show. And her husband, who owned a construction company, would be building a fake palm tree to put on the side of the stage while the girls danced. It was all part of the beach theme, she explained. She informed them that they would call the act the Beach Babes. The girls seemed to have no say in the matter.

The doorbell rang, and Anne's mom ran upstairs to answer it. In a minute, she came back down with a thin, bald guy with an earring.

"Girls, this is Sergei Propopotov, and he's going to help you with the dancing," Mrs. Zafian said. "You can call him Mr. Sergei. He's Russian. So he must be good, right?"

Julia was flabbergasted. She couldn't believe that Mrs. Zafian had hired a choreographer for the talent show.

"Okay, girls, listen up," Mr. Sergei said, clapping his hands, "I want you to get in two lines and do as I do. One, two, three . . ."

Mrs. Zafian went upstairs, and Mr. Sergei taught the girls a fairly simple routine with a few spins, jumps, and kicks. Thanks to years of dance classes, Julia was able to mirror his steps and lipsynch with the music easily. But it didn't take long for her to realize that the other girls were *terrible*. Jenny, in particular, seemed to have no sense of rhythm. She stumbled around trying to keep up, but she kept bumping into everybody and she seemed to not even know her left from her right. The girls thought it was all hilarious.

After fifteen minutes, Mrs. Zafian came back downstairs to see how things were going. She watched what they were doing for a few minutes, then turned off the music. There was an angry look on her face.

"Sergei," she said, "why is *my* daughter in the back row?"

"*Somebody* must be in the back row, Mrs. Zafian," Mr. Sergei explained.

"The somebody doesn't have to be my daughter."

"It's fine, Mom!" shouted Anne. "I don't care."

Mr. Sergei turned away, thinking Mrs. Zafian would just drop it. Nobody could possibly be so petty as to care which row their daughter was in. But Mrs. Zafian was used to getting her way.

"I'm paying you fifty dollars an hour!" she said, raising her voice. "I'm paying for the expensive costumes and the props. I won't have my daughter stand in the back where nobody can see her."

Mr. Sergei turned slowly, trying to think of a diplomatic way to smooth over the problem.

"The girls will be moving back and forth," he said. "Your daughter will sometimes be in the back row, and sometimes in the front row."

"I want her to be in the front row *all* the time," insisted Mrs. Zafian.

Mr. Sergei closed his eyes for a moment and rubbed his forehead. Then he threw his hands in the air.

"I cannot work under these conditions," he muttered as he gathered up his things. "Go get yourself another choreographer!"

"Fine!" Mrs. Zafian said. "Get out!"

Mr. Sergei stormed up the steps.

"Your girls dance like elephants!" he yelled as he slammed the door.

Everybody just stared at one another. Nobody said a word for a long time. It would be hard to replace Mr. Sergei. There wasn't exactly a long list of choreographers within driving distance of Cape Bluff, Kansas.

"What are we gonna do now?" Jessie asked.

"Maybe we should just forget about the act," said Chloe. "It was a dumb idea. Who are we kidding? We can't dance."

"I bet Julia could choreograph our routine," Anne said. "She can dance. She would be great."

"Would you be willing to do that, Julia?" asked Mrs. Zafian.

"Please please please please please?" begged the girls.

"Uh, I guess so," Julia replied. It's nice to be wanted.

When Julia showed up for the next rehearsal, all the Beach Babes were there except for Jenny.

"Jenny isn't feeling well," Anne's mom explained.

Julia ran the remaining girls through the routine, simplifying it so everybody would be able to do the steps. She was careful to put Anne in the front row.

When it was time to take a break, Mrs. Zafian came downstairs with a plate of cookies.

"You Beach Babes are starting to look really *good*," she said cheerfully. "Julia is a terrific choreographer. And if you ask me, Jenny was holding you girls back. It's nothing against her, of course. But maybe you should think about, you know, thinning out the herd."

"You mean we should kick Jenny out of the group?" Katie asked.

"Well, I wouldn't put it *that* way," Mrs. Zafian said.

"Jenny will be really upset," Anne said. "She's been my friend since we were little."

"I'm sure she'll understand, sweetie," Mrs. Zafian assured Anne. "This is part of life. You know, survival of the fittest. I'm sure Jenny has some other talent she's really good at. But the girl just can't dance. You saw her. It was just pathetic to watch."

The next morning at school, Julia saw Jenny in the hall.

"Are you feeling better, Jenny?" she asked.

"What do you mean?" Jenny replied. "I feel fine."

"Why didn't you come to rehearsal last night?" Julia said. "I heard you were sick."

"Sick?" Jenny said. "I wasn't sick. Anne's mom called and told me practice was canceled."

"Oh . . ."

Julia realized right away she had said the wrong thing. She shouldn't have said a word to Jenny.

"So I've been kicked out of the group?" Jenny asked, her hands on her hips. "Is that it?"

"I didn't mean—" Julia was tongue-tied.

Anne came over. She saw that Jenny was upset, on the verge of tears.

"What's the matter, Jenny?" Anne asked, putting an arm around her.

"Julia just told me I'm out of the group," Jenny said, wiping her eyes. "Oh, I get it. She's a better dancer than I am, so she's in and I'm out. Is that it? I guess our friendship means nothing. Fine!"

Jenny turned on her heel and stormed away, crying.

Now it was Anne who was mad. At Julia.

"Why did you tell Jenny we were kicking her out of the act?" she accused Julia.

"I didn't tell her!" Julia said. "I just asked her why she wasn't at rehearsal. She told me your mom called her and told her it was canceled."

"Why didn't you just keep your mouth shut?" Anne asked. "It wasn't any of your business."

The bell rang and as the girls went to their classes, Julia was totally confused. She wasn't used to playing head games with people. She had never mastered the fine art of lying and withholding information. Maybe Anne was going to kick her out of the group too.

At lunch, Julia went to sit at another table, but Anne waved her to come over. Nobody said a word about the situation with Jenny. It was like it never happened. But Julia saw that Jenny was sitting with some other girls at another table, glaring at her.

At the next rehearsal, the Beach Babes were still pretty awful. None of them could dance, and they weren't trying very hard either. They kept stopping to eat potato chips and answer their cell phones. The music was getting annoying to listen to. As she watched the girls stumble around, Julia thought she would have been better off if she had turned down Anne's offer to be part of the group. But it was too late now. She made a commitment to dance and do choreography for the Beach Babes.

Every day leading up to auditions, it was tense in the lunchroom. Anne would invite Julia to sit at her table, and Jenny would sit a few tables away, glaring at them.

Finally, on Friday, Jenny came over at the end of lunch and stood right in front of Julia at the popular girls' table.

"I've got news for you," she told the group. "I'm doing my *own* act with my *real* friends. It's going to be *ten* times better than your stupid Beach Babes routine. And I'm going to win the talent show!"

Chapter 8
Don Potash

When the tornado ripped his house off its foundation and flung it aside like a used tissue, Don was shaken up pretty badly. For a couple of hours, he was in shock, and barely spoke to anybody. But after a few days, when his family moved in with his cousins and life returned to something close to normal, Don regained his composure and his sense of humor.

That was a relief to everybody, because it was comedy that Don loved more than anything else. For his ninth birthday, he got a subscription to *Mad* magazine from his father, because that's what *he* used to read as a kid. From there, Don moved on to *Saturday Night Live, Monty Python's*

Flying Circus, *Seinfeld* reruns, *The Daily Show*, and just about anything else that was on Comedy Central. He loved to laugh. He would beg his parents to let him stay up to watch Jay Leno and David Letterman do their monologues. He was addicted to classic sitcoms like *The Honeymooners* and *Get Smart*. Instead of buying CDs and DVDs of the latest pop stars, Don collected old masters like Redd Foxx and Milton Berle, as well as newer comics like Jim Gaffigan and Chris Rock. He would spend hours watching stand-up comedy on TV.

Don had an old cassette tape recorder that he would hold up to the TV and record comedians he particularly liked. Then he would listen to them again in his bed at night, writing down the funniest lines in his comedy notebook. This way, he could memorize their routines and get the timing of the jokes just right. He learned that a joke could sometimes be much funnier if there was a millisecond pause between the setup and the punchline.

And yet, Don never thought about becoming a comedian himself someday. He was a quiet kid, for the most part. He didn't like to be the center of attention, and couldn't imagine getting up on a stage and telling jokes to an audience. He just loved to watch and listen to good comedy.

One day, in fourth grade, Don was sitting in class and his teacher passed around a box of crayons. She told the students to color in their worksheets while she stepped out of the room for a few minutes. Don picked out several different crayons, and noticed that the words "non-toxic" were on the crayon box.

"Non-toxic?" he asked the kids sitting at his table. "What does that mean?"

"It means that you won't die if you eat it," one of them replied.

"You won't *die*?" Don asked. "Are there actually kids who eat crayons? Why would anybody even *think* of eating a crayon? Those kids must be *really* hungry. But who would be so hungry that they'd put a crayon in their mouth and eat it?"

A few of the kids at his table started snickering, which encouraged him.

"Hey," he continued, "do you think the kids who eat crayons care what color crayons they eat? I wonder if different-colored crayons taste different? Like, are there some kids who eat only burnt sienna, and other kids whose favorite flavor is aquamarine?"

Don wasn't really trying to do comedy. He was just talking about something he noticed, and saying what popped into his head about it. But the other kids at the table couldn't stop giggling.

At first, Don thought they were laughing at him. But then he realized they were laughing *with* him. And it felt good. The laughter was a little reward, like when you're in first grade and the teacher puts a gold star on your paper.

"You're funny," the girl sitting across from him said.

"No, I'm completely serious," Don continued. "Like, what if four kids were sitting in the lunchroom. One of them opens up his lunch box and pulls out a peanut butter and jelly sandwich. The second kid pulls out a tuna sandwich. The third kid pulls out a turkey sandwich. And the fourth kid opens his lunch box and pulls out a big box of Crayolas."

"You should be a comedian," the girl said, laughing. Kids at some of the other tables were paying attention too.

Don couldn't resist. He chose one of the crayons from the box, put it in his mouth, and took a bite out of it. Jaws dropped open.

"Mmmm," he said, "Periwinkle. My favorite

color. I mean, flavor!" Then he grabbed his chest and fell to the floor, moaning, "I'm dying! I'm dying! I thought these were supposed to be non-toxic!"

He was just making it up off the top of his head, but the other kids in the class were falling all over themselves. They couldn't believe he had actually taken a bite out of a crayon.

"Thank you," Don said, as he got up off the floor and took a bow. "You've been a wonderful audience. Drive home safely."

When the teacher returned to the room, the class was giving Don a standing ovation.

Don went home that night and decided to try and write a stand-up comedy routine from scratch. He sat at the desk in his bedroom, took out a pen and paper, and started to brainstorm. But nothing happened. No brilliant ideas popped into his head. He couldn't think of anything funny. Writing comedy was *hard*.

He looked at his desk. There wasn't a whole lot to see. Scotch tape. A stapler. Erasers. A ruler. Glue sticks. A pencil sharpener. So he started jotting down a few notes about the stuff on his desk.

You wouldn't think that school supplies could be all that funny. But it was really no different from Jerry Seinfeld talking about doing his laundry. Professional comedians find the humor in everyday things that are obvious, but nobody ever talks about. Humor is everywhere. *Anything* can be funny. Staplers and glue sticks can be *hilarious*.

If a tree falls in the forest and no one is around to hear it, does it make a sound? If a joke is told and no one is around to hear it, is it funny? Don had no idea whether or not his little routine about school supplies was any good. The only way to find out would be to try it in front of an audience.

The next morning at school, a bunch of kids were crowded around a desk near the office. Don went over to see what the excitement was all about. It was the sign-up sheet for the talent show. Just about everybody, it seemed, wanted to be part of it. Kids were signing up to sing, dance, play musical instruments, do magic tricks, juggle, and so on.

Don shook his head. Just about every kid in sixth grade signed up to do *something*. He knew that all those kids didn't have talent. A lot of them had no business being in a talent show. They just wanted to show off, he figured, and be on stage.

Don looked down the list of names. A lot of different talents were represented, but no comedians. He thought it over for a minute, and finally picked up the pen. What the heck. On one of the bottom lines, he wrote:

DON POTASH, COMEDIAN

Over the next few days, Don spent hours rehearsing his school supply routine in front of the mirror in his bedroom. He inserted pauses in the spots where he thought the audience would laugh. When everything felt smooth, he clocked it. It came out to four and a half minutes—more than twice as long as the two-minute limit.

He sat down and carefully edited out the lines he didn't think were that funny. It wasn't easy. But when he was done, he had a good, tight, two-minute routine with no dead spots. It may not have been as funny as Jerry Seinfeld, but it wasn't bad. Don performed it over and over again in front of the mirror until he had it memorized.

He was ready.

Chapter 9

Richard Ackoon

For his eighth birthday, Richard's parents gave him his most treasured present—a rhyming dictionary.

Regular dictionaries are simply alphabetical, of course, listing words and providing origins, definitions, and synonyms for them. A rhyming dictionary lists *sounds* in alphabetical order, and provides words that rhyme with those sounds.

So, for instance, if you looked up the sound "each," a rhyming dictionary would give you "beach," "bleach," "breech," "leach," "peach," "preach," "reach," "screech," "speech," "teach," "beseech," "impeach," "outreach," "Long Beach," and other words that rhyme with "each."

Rhyming dictionaries are used by poets and songwriters. And rappers.

Richard's parents had mixed feelings about giving him a rhyming dictionary. On one hand, they were thrilled to hear that their son wanted a *book* for his birthday instead of a video game or some silly toy he would get tired of in five minutes. They wanted to encourage his longtime interest in reading, words, and language.

On the other hand, they didn't like the sounds they heard coming out of his bedroom. 50 Cent. Xzibit. Jay Z. Notorious B.I.G. Richard's favorite singers had names that didn't even *look* like names. He had developed an unhealthy interest in rap music, his parents feared.

They weren't dummies. They followed the news. Rappers were always showing off their cars and their guns, getting arrested, having violent feuds with each other, disrespecting women, and abusing drugs. Mr. and Mrs. Ackoon didn't want their son mixed up with that stuff. He was only in third grade!

When Richard started getting interested in rap music, his parents tried to push him in the direction of country, rock, pop, jazz, blues, and even show music. But none of it clicked with him.

"I don't *care* about the music," he kept telling them. "All I care about are the words."

Richard tried to explain to his parents that just because he liked rap music didn't mean he was going to grow up to be like one of those rappers who set a bad example for kids.

"Your favorite singer is Johnny Cash," he would tell his father. "Did you ever shoot a man in Reno just to watch him die?"

"That's different," Mr. Ackoon argued. "Johnny Cash never shot anybody. He just wrote that in a song. But those rappers you listen to actually go around shooting each other."

"Hardly any of 'em do that, Dad!"

Richard claimed that *anything* can be used in a good way or a bad way. He told his dad that a knife could be used to cut the food on your plate, or it could be used to stab somebody. A rapper could use words to insult a person, or they could use words to raise millions of dollars for charity. He could use words in a positive way, he explained. He could actually make the world better by rapping. His parents doubted it.

But Richard didn't seem like an angry kid who

would ever break the law or hurt anybody. He didn't have an angry bone in his body. So his parents agreed to buy him the rhyming dictionary for his birthday. But they were never really able to understand why he liked rap music or wanted to be a rapper.

"That stuff doesn't even *sound* like music!" his father would argue.

The other kids at school were also a little mystified by Richard's interest in rap. Like almost everybody in Cape Bluff, Richard was not African American. There *had been* a few well-known white rappers—Eminem, The Beastie Boys—but there was still something odd about seeing a white kid rap, especially a short white kid in third grade who had red hair, freckles, and braces.

There were a lot of people who felt that a white kid didn't even have the *right* to rap. Rappers had to come from "the hood" and have "street cred." They had to pay their dues. They had to be oppressed.

Richard didn't think that was fair. Words were words. *Anybody* should be allowed to use them. Your skin color shouldn't determine what you could or couldn't say. That was what free speech and equal rights were all about.

And besides, Richard felt he *did* pay his dues, just by living in Cape Bluff. While it was true that he had never witnessed gang violence or the kinds of things poor kids growing up in the inner city experience, he had seen some bad things. Like his town being ripped apart by a tornado. That was pretty bad. Like people living in their cars because their houses were destroyed. Like friends who came over to his house not to hang out, but because they knew they could get something to eat there. Everyone in Cape Bluff had experienced poverty and hard times firsthand.

The other birthday present that Richard cherished came from his grandparents—a drum machine.

The Micro Rhythm Trak was a silver box no larger than a big piece of cake. It had twenty buttons on it. By pressing the buttons in different combinations, you could simulate virtually any drumbeat in any tempo, and create new ones as well. If you plugged the drum machine into an amplifier or decent set of speakers and closed your eyes, you would never know it wasn't a real drummer playing. His grandparents bought the Micro Rhythm Trak on eBay for forty dollars.

Richard didn't care about winning a Hummer. He didn't even know what a Hummer *was*. At eight years old, being able to drive a car seemed like something that would happen in the next *century*. But the night he found out about the talent show, Richard went home and shut himself in his room. He climbed into bed with a pad and paper, took out his rhyming dictionary, and turned on the drum machine. He punched in a beat that felt right, nodded his head with the rhythm, and started brainstorming.

He thought about what had happened to the people of Cape Bluff, and what was going to happen next. When words started coming into his head, he scribbled them down on the pad as quickly as he could. The rhymes came fast. He only had to use the rhyming dictionary in a few cases. Sometimes the words just flow.

Once he had the basic structure of his rap down, he tinkered with it, changing a word here or there, crossing out lyrics that didn't fit, and inserting replacements. He didn't even notice that two hours flew by until his mother knocked on the door and told him it was bedtime.

"One minute, Mom!"

Richard looked at what he had written. There was always room for improvement, of course, but it was good. *Really* good. He read it one more time from start to finish, changing just a few words to make the syllables fit the beat perfectly. He turned off the drum machine and smiled.

He was going to blow them away at the auditions.

Chapter 10

The Kid's Got Talent

Whether it was making a peanut butter and jelly sandwich or running a talent show, when Mary Marotta decided to do something, she did it *right*.

In the four days leading up to the Friday night auditions, Mrs. Marotta was a ball of energy. She put flyers up in the windows of every Cape Bluff store. She got in touch with Mr. Linn, the man who offered to donate his sound and lighting equipment. She had to make sure the custodian would be around to open the school on Friday. She had to make sure there would be enough hand sanitizer and toilet paper in the bathrooms. She had to deal with pushy parents who thought their amazing child was the second coming of Judy

Garland. She had to deal with whiny third graders who couldn't decide if they should sing "You Are My Sunshine" or "I'm A Little Teapot." It seemed like there were a million details to nail down. She knew that if she didn't do it, it wouldn't get done.

Mrs. Marotta even found the time to write a letter to Justin Chanda in care of his lawyer in New York. It was a long shot, but maybe Cape Bluff's most famous talent might be willing to come home and make a surprise appearance at the talent show for the sake of the town. It couldn't hurt to ask.

After dinner on Friday, Mrs. Marotta dropped Elsie and Edward off at the babysitter's house and drove to Cape Bluff Elementary School for the auditions. As she was parking her car on the blacktop, she noticed a group of boys shooting hoops on the old rusted backboard in the corner. She watched them for a minute, recognizing a sixth grader named Tyler Harvey who lived in her neighborhood. Sometimes he came around to rake leaves or shovel snow in order to earn money.

"Hey, Tyler," Mrs. Marotta shouted, "are you and your friends going to audition for the talent show?"

"No, thanks, Mrs. Marotta," he said, snickering for the benefit of the other boys.

"Talent shows are lame," one of them said.

"Yeah," said another. "That stuff is for girls."

"No, it's not," said Mrs. Marotta. "Lots of guys are going to be participating."

"Oh, yeah?" Tyler said. "Like who?"

Mrs. Marotta looked at the list on her clipboard.

"Paul Crichton and his band The BluffTones are going to be in it," she said. "Then there's Cutter Whitley, A. J. Campinha, Cole Roberts, Chris Flint. We've also got a rapper named Richard Ackoon and a singer named Aidan Baker. There will be lots of other boys too."

"I'm not getting up on a stage and singing some stupid song," one of the guys said.

"Me neither," said another.

"You don't have to sing," Mrs. Marotta told them. "You can do anything you'd like."

"No, thanks," said Tyler. "We like to play ball. We don't do put on shows."

Mrs. Marotta shrugged, got her bag out of the trunk, and started walking toward the school. Then she stopped and turned around to look at Tyler again. He had a point. There *were* more girls auditioning for the show than boys. The show really needed some more guys in it, and more variety of acts too. Besides, she had a feeling that Tyler and his friends would really *like* to be part of the show, but they were embarrassed. Probably in their eyes, singing and dancing just weren't cool. Or manly.

"What if I gave you guys costumes to wear?" she shouted to the boys.

"What kind of costumes?" Tyler asked.

"I know they have some gorilla suits backstage from the school play last year," she told them. "Nobody will see your faces."

"Gorillas are cool," one of the boys said.

"And we don't have to sing?" Tyler asked.

"No."

"Do we have to dance?" asked Tyler.

"Nope," Mrs. Marotta said. "Like I said, you can do whatever you want. You can be basketball-playing gorillas for all I care. Come on, it'll be fun."

"Well . . . okay," Tyler said, "as long as we don't have to sing or dance."

Tyler and his friends followed Mrs. Marotta into the school. She told them where to find the gorilla suits in a closet backstage.

The multipurpose room was already filling up with children and parents who arrived early. Some kids were putting on costumes they had made or were lugging elaborate props they had built.

As more people arrived, the noise level gradually went up until it reached the point where you could accurately call it a commotion. Kids were running around like crazy, which is what kids tend to do when they're unsupervised. Mrs. Marotta fully expected it. That's why she brought a whistle and a bullhorn in her bag.

An ear-piercing whistle filled the room.

"Attention!" she bellowed into the bullhorn. "Quiet! Ah, that's better. Everybody sit down, please!"

Everyone sat down. Mrs. Marotta wasn't sure if it was because she had yelled at them or because they noticed that the panel of judges had arrived—Mayor Rettino, Principal Anderson, and Reverend Mercun. Honest Dave Gale had walked into the room too.

"Who's gonna win my Hummer?" he asked everyone cheerfully.

Mrs. Marotta posted the list of acts on the wall and announced that she would call each act to the stage one at a time, so students should listen for their names. She also requested that everyone be quiet and respectful of the person on the stage. Performing in front of an audience was a very difficult thing to do, Mrs. Marotta told them. It took a lot of courage to get up on a stage and be judged by other people.

She called out for a boy named Jimmy, a quiet little third grader. He climbed up on the stage with a violin and played Beethoven's "Violin Sonata Number 7 in C Minor." It was obvious that he had been playing for years, and he received a nice round of applause from the kids and their parents in the audience.

"Very nice, Jimmy," Mrs. Marotta said as the three judges gave him the thumbs-up and words of encouragement.

None of the kids knew this, but from the start Mrs. Marotta and Principal Anderson had agreed that the talent show would *not* be just like the popular TV show *American Idol*. There would be judges and a grand prize—the Hummer—of course. But nobody would be rejected. Any child who wanted to could participate, no matter how awful their act was. Nobody would be criticized, poked fun at, humiliated, kicked off an island, voted out, or made to feel bad. The talent show was supposed to be a positive experience, not a negative one.

After Jimmy went back to his seat with his violin, a sixth-grade girl in a wheelchair sang an off-key version of "Under the Sea" from *The Little Mermaid*. She was followed by four cheerleaders who threw one another up in the air, a boy who played a lovely Chopin sonata on the piano, a trio of Irish step dancers, and two boys who did the old Abbott and Costello "Who's on First?" routine. Or tried to, anyway, until they got confused and forgot the name of the third baseman ("I Don't Know").

"Very good," Mrs. Marotta yelled into the bullhorn after each act had reached its two-minute time limit. Next!"

Some of the acts were very good. Elke Villa, as expected, was amazing. She sang "Over the Rainbow" from *The Wizard of Oz*, and a few of the grownups who were hanging around were all misty-eyed. The little third grader, Richard Ackoon, did what he called his "Cape Bluff Rap #1." As he predicted, he blew the audience away.

Other acts weren't quite as polished. A young juggler tried to keep three clubs spinning in the air, but he kept dropping them. A magician pulled a rabbit out of a hat, but it was obvious that the rabbit had been stashed in the box that was right under the hat. It was also obvious that the rabbit was a stuffed animal. A ventriloquist had a really lifelike dummy, but the dummy's voice sounded just like the ventriloquist's, whose mouth was moving.

Then there were the acts that were just plain *weird*.

A nerdy-looking boy named Ricky got up on stage. He didn't have any props, instrument, or prerecorded music.

"What's your talent, Ricky?" asked Mrs. Marotta. "You didn't write it on the sign-up sheet."

"I do impersonations," he replied. "I will now do my impersonation of a piece of bacon frying."

Ricky got down on the floor. First he started shaking. Then he slithered around the stage and slowly pulled his legs in to make it look like his body was shrinking. The whole time, he was making sizzling noises. It actually *did* look a little bit like bacon frying. The judges gave him a nice round of applause.

Next, a girl named Amy got on the stage holding a short stick and a ball of yarn.

"What's your talent?" asked Mrs. Marotta.

"I am going to crochet," she said.

"Did you say you're going to play croquet?" asked Reverend Mercun in the front row.

"No, I'm going to *crochet*," Amy repeated.

She sat down on a chair and started pulling loops of yarn through the other loops.

"It's not the same as knitting," Amy said as she worked. "You don't use two needles, and only one loop is active at a time."

The judges watched her for two minutes, and put their heads together to discuss things.

"I have to admit it," said Mayor Rettino. "The kid's got talent."

"You're in, Amy," said Principal Anderson.

The next contestant, a boy named Eric, climbed up on the stage carrying a laptop computer.

"What's your talent, Eric?" asked Mrs. Marotta.

"I'm going to do a PowerPoint presentation," he announced.

The judges put their heads together to talk things over.

"I'm sure your PowerPoint is wonderful, but I'm not sure that it qualifies as a *talent*," said Mayor Rettino.

"How come that girl before me was allowed to knit, but I can't do my PowerPoint?" asked Eric.

"It wasn't knitting!" Amy yelled from the back of the room. "It was crocheting!"

"We have to draw the line somewhere," said Reverend Mercun. "We're really sorry."

"Fine!" Eric said, and he left in a huff.

While the other acts were performing at the front of the stage, The BluffTones were told to set up their drum set and other equipment. Paul Crichton gave a copy of the "Stacy's Mom" lyrics to Mrs. Marotta, as required by the talent show rules.

"One . . . two . . . three . . . four!" Paul called out.

Stacy's mom has got it going on.
Stacy's mom has got it going on.
Stacy's mom has got it going on.
Stacy's mom has got it going on.

The band ran through the song without missing a note. All the kids, who had been fidgeting during the other acts, stopped and stared at The

BluffTones. Toes were tapping. Heads were bobbing. By the second verse, some of the kids were
up and dancing.

I know it might be wrong, but I'm in love with Stacy's mom.

Paul hit the last chord and looked up. They
had totally nailed it. Kids were clapping and whistling. The BluffTones took a deep bow. Clearly,
Elke Villa had some competition on her hands.

The panel of judges—Mayor Rettino, Reverend
Mercun, and Principal Anderson—had a brief
whispered conversation.

"Excuse me," Mayor Rettino said. "Will you
boys come over here, please?"

Paul, Jim, Victor, and Rob put down their
instruments and hopped off the stage confidently.
They figured the judges were going to tell them
how great they sounded. Reverend Mercun was
looking at the lyric sheet to "Stacy's Mom."

"Guys," Principal Anderson said, "you're terrific, but I'm very sorry to tell you that you can't
sing that song in the talent show."

"Why not?" Paul asked. "Is somebody else
doing it?"

"No . . . ," the principal said.

"I find that song to be . . . suggestive," said Reverend Mercun.

"Huh?" Jim asked. "Suggestive of *what*?"

"Are you saying the song is dirty?" asked Paul.

"The singer is in love with his girlfriend's mother," explained the Reverend.

"Yeah, so?" asked Rob.

"Well, that's inappropriate," Reverend Mercun said.

"Are you kidding me?" Paul said, his voice rising. "It's just a song. It's *funny*."

"So just because *you* think it's dirty . . . ," said Rob.

Victor shot them a look to get them to shut up. You don't talk back to grown-ups. Especially when one of them is a reverend.

"We could play 'Satisfaction,'" Jim said.

"The song by The Rolling Stones?" asked Reverend Mercun. "That's suggestive too."

"What's suggestive about it?" Paul asked. "That's ridiculous!

"How about 'Wild Thing'?" asked Rob.

"That song is also quite suggestive," said

Reverend Mercun. "There must be something else you boys can play that wouldn't offend anyone."

"'Stacy's Mom' won't offend anyone!" Paul said. "It was a big hit. It was on the radio. It was in a Dr Pepper commercial!"

"Why don't you fellows play 'Wipeout'?" suggested Mayor Rettino. "I heard you played that at a birthday party recently. The kids loved it. And it doesn't have any offensive lyrics."

"It doesn't have any lyrics at *all*!" Paul pointed out.

"We're not playing 'Wipeout,'" Victor said firmly. "*Anybody* can play 'Wipeout.'"

"I'm terribly sorry," Reverend Mercun told the boys, "but the talent show has to maintain certain standards of decency. There will be lots of parents and grandparents in the audience. I'm sure you understand."

"I don't understand!" Rob said.

"Come on, guys," said Victor. "Let's get out of here. We don't need this."

"Hang on," Paul said. "Can we have a minute? Band meeting."

The BluffTones went off to the side of the

stage and huddled up like a football team.

"This is bull, man," said Victor. "They can keep their stupid talent show. We don't have to take this."

"What are we supposed to do about it?" asked Jim.

"What if we changed the words?" Rob suggested. "Like, 'Stacy's Mom is the bomb.'"

"That's lame," said Paul, "and it doesn't have the right number of syllables, either."

"'Stacy's Mom can really sing a psalm,'" said Victor, which made everybody crack up.

Paul took a minute to think things over. His dad had told him a lot about rock and roll history. He had learned one thing—nobody ever got famous in music by following the rules. They said a white guy couldn't sing black music, and then Elvis came along. They said guitar groups were on the way out, and then The Beatles came along. They said you should treat your instruments with love and care, and The Who and Jimi Hendrix came along and destroyed them right on stage. They said rock music was dead and played out, and then along came punk, heavy metal, and rap.

The way to get famous, Paul decided, isn't to do what you're told. If you want to be famous, you break the rules and piss off the powers that be. Rock and roll is about freedom and rebellion. If he compromised now, when his career hadn't even started yet, he would be compromising for the rest of his life. This was a moment of truth, a turning point.

So he came up with an idea.

"Okay, here's what we're gonna do," Paul told the band. "We tell them we'll play *another* song. Whatever they want to hear. 'Row, Row, Row Your Boat.' I don't care. Then, on the night of the talent show, we get up on stage and do 'Stacy's Mom.' That will blow their minds!"

"We're gonna get in trouble, Paul," said Jim. "You know that, right?"

"Good," Paul said. "Let's get in trouble! Let's be rebels."

"Yeah, what are they gonna do?" asked Victor. "Suspend us?"

"Let 'em," Paul said. "We'll be rock and roll outlaws."

"Okay," Rob agreed, hesitantly. "I'm in. Let's do it."

The BluffTones broke their huddle and went back to talk with the judges.

"So what's it going to be, boys?" asked Principal Anderson.

"Put us down for 'Wipeout,'" Paul said.

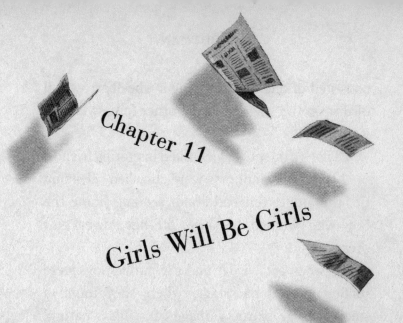

Chapter 11

Girls Will Be Girls

Tyler and his basketball-playing gorillas found that, indeed, *lots* of boys were auditioning to be in the talent show. A group of ten fourth-grade Elvis impersonators danced to Michael Jackson's "Thriller." The kids in the crowd seemed to really enjoy a bunch of guys dressed as penguins riding fake surfboards while strumming fake guitars to the theme song from *Hawaii Five-O*. Where they found a dozen penguin costumes was anybody's guess. They even had a fake igloo as a prop.

Probably the lamest act was a group of five boys who called themselves "The Janitors." They came out on stage dressed in overalls and holding brooms. There was no music. The entire act consisted of one boy dumping a wheelbarrow full of dirt on the stage, and the other four sweeping it up.

"That's a talent?" Tyler asked his gorilla friends.

After The Janitors were finished cleaning up, the judges felt bad about sending home the boy who wanted to show off his PowerPoint presentation.

Between acts, Tyler and the gorilla boys were milling around backstage, where they found a stack of large plastic garbage cans. It's a natural fact that if you combine three or more sixth-grade boys, garbage cans, and time on their hands, it invariably adds up to one thing—drumming.

The boys began to beat on the garbage cans with their hands, and they didn't notice how loud they were until Mrs. Marotta suddenly came backstage to see what was going on.

They stopped beating on the garbage cans instantly.

"Sorry, Mrs. Marotta," said Tyler.

"Sorry, nothing," she replied. "That's going to be your act!"

The Drumming Gorillas were born.

It's human nature. Boys like to beat on garbage cans, and girls like to dance. Julia Maguire, Anne Zafian, and the other Beach Babes walked into the multipurpose room a half hour late for the audition. Partly it was because they had a hard time fitting the fake palm tree prop into Anne's mom's minivan. But the other reason was that Mrs. Zafian wanted the girls to make a grand entrance.

And they did. With matching bathing suits, hairstyles, and sunglasses, it was hard to miss the Beach Babes. When the popular girls entered a room, everybody always stopped what they were doing to watch.

"Sorry we're late," Mrs. Zafian said breezily. "Can the Beach Babes still do their act?"

Mrs. Marotta was annoyed, but she tried not to show it. She knew that Mrs. Zafian got pleasure out of ruffling people's feathers.

"Of course," Mrs. Marotta said. "Go ahead. It's your turn anyway."

Anne's dad lugged in the palm tree he had built and set it up on the stage. The girls got into position. Electronic hip-hop beach music came out of the speakers, and the Beach Babes did their lip synch dance number.

There's just one word to describe this act. It was awful. Just *awful*. The girls were stumbling around, bumping into one another, completely out of rhythm. Their fancy set, colorful costumes, and professional music couldn't disguise the fact that these girls had zero talent.

Except for Julia Maguire, of course. After six years of ballet lessons, she could hardly believe she had agreed to join this group just so she could be with the popular girls. She wanted to hide her face while they were dancing.

When the Beach Babes finished their horrible act, the back door of the multipurpose room opened and *another* group of girls came in. They were led by Jenny, the girl who had been kicked out of the Beach Babes. And like the Beach Babes, this group had matching bathing suits, sunglasses, and a fake palm tree. The tree, which was slightly bigger, was carried by Jenny's mother and Sergei Propopotov, the Russian choreographer.

"What's the name of this act?" asked Principal Anderson.

"We're the Sand Kittens!" Jenny announced.

"Hey, you stole our act!" Anne Zafian yelled at Jenny.

"What are you gonna do about it?" Jenny said. "Sue us?"

Mrs. Marotta rolled her eyes. She had seen a lot of spoiled, snot-nosed kids and overbearing parents in her time, but this topped them all. She didn't want to see a fight break out between the Beach Babes and the Sand Kittens, so she quickly instructed Jenny and her group to get up on stage and do their thing.

Well, the Sand Kittens were even *worse* than the Beach Babes, if that's possible. They couldn't dance. They couldn't even lip synch. And they sure couldn't dance and lip synch at the same time. One of them almost fell off the stage. But Jenny was smiling the whole time. She had gotten her revenge on Anne, and that was all that mattered.

A bunch of other acts followed. An accordion player. A girl doing rhythmic gymnastics. A mime. Somebody reciting poetry. A boy riding a unicycle. Some of the kids packed up their stuff and left after they had finished their audition. But most of them hung around to watch their friends and classmates.

Don Potash looked at the list of acts that was

posted on the wall. His name was almost at the bottom because he was one of the last to sign up.

He had been standing silently in the back of the multipurpose room the whole time watching the others perform. He saw Paul Crichton and The BluffTones sing "Stacy's Mom," only to be told the lyrics were not appropriate for tender young ears. He felt bad for them. Julia Maguire and her lip synching hip-hop dancers were simply awful, laughably untalented. Don felt bad for them, too.

But Don couldn't really pay close attention to *any* of the acts, because he was spending the whole time repeating his comedy routine in his head. He didn't want to mess up.

Why doesn't anyone else look nervous? Don thought to himself as he scanned the multipurpose room. Maybe everybody else had performed on stage before. He began biting his fingernails, something he did only when he was feeling pressure.

He wished there were no grown-ups in the room. Mrs. Marotta was a ball of energy, running around and telling kids what to do, where to stand, and when to go on. Mayor Rettino, Principal Anderson, and Reverend Mercun were sitting in the front row, whispering to one another after each act was finished. There was a big spotlight at the back of the room that was pointed at the stage.

Don wiped his palms on his pants. He had never felt this way before.

Finally, after almost all the acts had finished, Mrs. Marotta announced, "Don Potash, comedian? Don? Where's Don?"

"Here," Don said, raising his hand.

He wished she hadn't used the word "comedian." He just wanted to get up on stage and do his little bit to make the other kids laugh, like he had done in class with the non-toxic crayon bit. Once she said the word "comedian," everybody turned to look at him. Now he had to be funny. *I dare you to make me laugh,* they seemed to say.

Don had never performed in front of people before. This was all new. He had a severe case of flop sweat—a nervous condition brought on by the fear of failure. And he hadn't even said a word yet. His clothes were sticking to him.

He climbed the steps at the side of the empty stage. There was a microphone stand there. It occurred to Don that he had never spoken into a microphone before. He didn't know how far away he should put his mouth.

The lights were dimmed and the spotlight hit him in the face. He had never been in a spotlight before either, and was surprised at how blinding it was. He couldn't see anything, or anyone, in front of him. But he knew hundreds of kids were staring at him, waiting to hear what he had to say. Waiting to see if he could make them laugh.

"Go ahead, Don," Mrs. Marotta urged him when she saw his hesitancy. "Remember, two minutes. Quiet, everyone!"

There was silence. Don closed his eyes for a moment, took a deep breath, and thought of his opening line.

But it didn't come.

What *was* it? He searched his memory. His mind was a blank. Nothing. He closed his eyes again. His brain seemed to have stopped working. Sweat was pouring down his forehead, and getting in his eyes. We wiped it away with his sleeve. He was afraid he might pass out.

"You okay, Don?" asked Mrs. Marotta.

"I . . . uh . . ."

He was speechless. Frozen. Paralyzed.

"Want to try again later?" Mrs. Marotta suggested gently.

Don tried one last time to come up with the first line of his routine.

Nothing.

"No," he said. "I'm done."

Don Potash, humiliated, walked off the stage and ran all the way home.

Chapter 12

No Hard Feelings

It had been a long night. All together, more than thirty acts had auditioned for the talent show. Only two had been knocked off the original sign-up list—the kid with the PowerPoint, and Don Potash, the comedian who couldn't remember his routine.

It was close to eleven o'clock when the last audition was over. Mary Marotta was exhausted, and there would be a lot of work to do in the week leading up to the talent show. She had to recruit parents to act as ushers, chaperones, and, if necessary, disciplinarians. There were tickets and programs to be designed and printed. Ads to be sold. She had to contact the local media to ask them to cover the event. The cupcakes had to be coordinated to make sure there would be the right balance of chocolate and vanilla. And rehearsals after school every day, of course. There was no guarantee that everything would come together in time for the show. And of course, Mrs. Marotta had to prepare for that unexpected emergency that always seems to happen at the worst possible moment.

But all in all, she was feeling hopeful. Seeing the actual performers up on the stage made the talent show seem more real to everyone in the room. It was actually going to happen. Cape Bluff really *did* have talent. Elke Villa was awesome, as expected. The BluffTones were a tight band. A few of the singers could actually sing. Some of the dancers could actually dance. And there were a lot of other kids who had shown a surprising amount of talent.

As everyone left Cape Bluff Elementary School that night, they passed by the Hummer that was parked on the front lawn. It was anybody's to win.

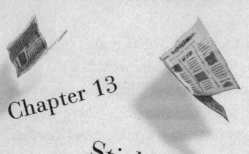

Chapter 13

Sticking It to the Man

"Let's go, people!" Mrs. Marotta bellowed at the top of her lungs. "Annie Oatman on stage right now. Pronto! Olive Howard and Megan Swick on deck. And K. C. Lynch is on double deck. Get ready, Tammy Russo. You're next. Keep it moving, you guys! Everybody else, stop the chitchat! Show some respect. Kids are working hard out here."

There was a week to go before the show. Mrs. Marotta scheduled rehearsals after school each day, and all participants had to be there. She seemed to be everywhere at once—backstage, out in the audience, in the hallway, and even in the parking lot soothing the nerves of anxious kids and parents. She had forgotten to bring along her bullhorn, and her throat was sore from shouting.

Thirty acts. Some needed more rehearsal than others. It wasn't easy shuttling singers and dancers and ventriloquists back and forth. There was a sense of barely controlled chaos. Some kids had to leave early for their soccer practices. Some kids got sick. Some parents were a nuisance. It was the usual whining you get whenever groups of people are together. Mrs. Marotta was tired and losing her voice, but also exhilarated. She hadn't had this much fun since she was in *Grease*, back in senior year of high school.

Paul and The BluffTones played "Wipeout" at rehearsal so many times they were wiped out. They could have played the song in their sleep. In fact, it almost *seemed* as though they were playing it in their sleep.

"Come on!" Mrs. Marotta yelled at them after one particularly lackluster run-through. "Put a little life into it, boys! The show is in a few days."

It was all an act anyway. The BluffTones had no intention of playing "Wipeout" at the talent show. But they had to keep practicing it anyway. They hadn't told anyone outside the band that they would actually be playing "Stacy's Mom." They had been rehearsing the song secretly at home. It was hard to keep the secret.

After the first couple of days, the kids were sick of rehearsing. Each act had just two minutes to do their thing on stage, but they had to spend the rest of the time sitting around, tuning up their instruments, eating snacks, doing homework, or just waiting for their turn. It was boring.

The Beach Babes and the Sand Kittens staked out positions in the back of the multipurpose room, as far away as possible from each other. No words were exchanged between the rival groups. Every so often one of the girls would take a peek or glare at the enemy, but other than that, no eye contact was made. It was like a cold war. Each group was convinced that they were better than the other. Neither group had any idea how embarrassingly bad they both truly were. The fact was that neither group had the slightest chance of winning the talent show.

Julia wasn't having any fun. She never fit in with the other Beach Babes. As they sat around gossiping about everybody and texting their friends, she became increasingly tired of being around them. All they cared about was the way they looked, the stuff they owned, and which boys they thought were cute. Julia wished she had never agreed to be in the Beach Babes. But she couldn't back out at this point. She was their choreographer. It wouldn't be right.

As the rehearsals dragged on, Julia would come up with more frequent excuses to go to the bathroom, get a drink of water, or just take a walk. Anything to get away from the other girls.

The BluffTones had set up a little beachhead behind the stage, where Victor's drum set was being stored. They couldn't jam, because everyone had to be quiet while rehearsals were going on. The other guys in the band liked to hang out with The Drumming Gorillas in the boys' bathroom, but Paul would sit on the floor next to the drum set talking with anybody who came by. He was a good talker, one of these kids who could effortlessly strike up a conversation with anyone, even a complete stranger.

He was chatting with one of the stage crew when Elke walked by. Things had been a little awkward between them ever since she turned down Paul's offer to join the band. When he noticed her, he waved her over. The kid on the stage crew said he had to go work on the scenery.

"Hey," Paul said to Elke. "I just wanted you to know that, well, I hope there are no hard feelings, y'know, about the band and everything. Good luck in the show. You're gonna be great."

"Hey, you too," she replied. "Thanks for saying that."

"You want some Skittles?" Paul asked. "My mom gave me this big bag of the stuff, and I don't even like 'em."

"Sure."

Elke sat on the floor next to Paul and took a handful of Skittles.

"Your band is really good," she said. "Maybe I *should* have joined when you asked me."

"Nah, you were right. You're better off singing solo," Paul told her. "The guitars and drums would only compete with your voice."

At that point, Julia walked by and took a drink from the water fountain. She glanced over and saw Paul and Elke talking.

"Hey, Beach Babe!" Paul called out.

"Yeah?"

Julia came over to where Paul and Elke were sitting on the floor.

"Why are you dancing with those losers?" Paul asked. Elke laughed.

"They're not losers," Julia said, chuckling.

"Actually, they're really popular," Elke said. "All the other girls wish they could be them."

"They're idiots," Paul insisted. "Bubble-brained morons. And except for Julia, they can't dance to save their lives. They should be in a *no*-talent show."

Julia covered her mouth and shushed Paul as she giggled. She didn't want the rest of the Beach Babes to hear.

"I don't know what I was thinking when I joined them," she whispered. "It seemed like a good idea at the time."

"Why don't you hang with us?" Paul said. "We've got Skittles."

"I love Skittles!" Julia said, parking herself on the floor next to Elke and reaching into the bag.

"Are you really friends with those girls?" Elke asked Julia. "You don't seem like their type."

"They asked me to dance with them, so I said yes," Julia replied.

"If they asked you to jump off the Brooklyn Bridge, would you?" said Paul. "That's what my dad always says to me."

The boys' bathroom was right down the hall, and Richard Ackoon came out of it. Not many third graders had signed up to be in the talent show, so he was one of the youngest kids there, and the only rapper. He saw Paul sitting on the floor eating candy with Elke and Julia. Richard was a little intimidated by the older kids and didn't usually talk to them. But he *really* liked candy.

"Are those M&M's?" he asked, hinting that he wanted some.

"Do you like M&M's?" Paul replied.

"Yeah!"

"Well, they're not M&M's," Paul told him. "They're Skittles."

"I *love* Skittles!" Richard said.

"You want some?" Paul asked.

"Sure!"

"What grade are you in?"

"Third," Richard replied.

"Oh, too bad," Paul told him. "You can't have any. The Skittles are for fourth graders and up."

Richard pouted. He looked like he might cry.

"Oh, give him some!" Elke and Julia said, reaching for the bag.

"I'm just goofing on you, dude!" Paul told Richard. "Come on, sit down and have some Skittles with us. Your rap is cool. But you gotta get yourself a cool rap name. Like P. Diddy or R. Kelly. 'Richard' is no name for a rapper."

"How about R. Ackoon?" suggested Elke.

"Raccoon!" said Julia.

"Yeah!" Paul said. "From now on, we're gonna call you Raccoon. The rapping raccoon."

Richard liked the name, and he liked the attention from the older kids too. He flopped on the floor next to the drums, taking a big handful of Skittles and slapping it into his mouth.

"Hey, do you guys ever get scared?" Richard asked the others.

"Scared of what, Raccoon?" Paul said.

"Y'know. Getting up there," Richard said. "I never rapped in front of an audience before. With all those people watching. It's scary."

"You'll be fine," Paul assured him. "Relax, Raccoon. You're a natural rapper."

"The first time I sang in public," Elke told the others, "I puked my guts up backstage before

I went on. I was so scared that I thought I was going to faint."

"Oh, great," Richard said. "That's what I'll probably do."

"Do you still get nervous?" Julia asked Elke.

"A little," she replied. "But each time I sing in public, it's easier."

"It's probably good to be *little* scared," Paul said. "Keeps you on your toes."

"I could never do what you do, Elke," Julia said. "Just get up there all by myself. I could never dance in front of an audience unless there were other girls dancing with me. I don't want everybody staring at me."

"Oh, you could do it if you tried," Elke told her. "You just have to pretend that the audience isn't there."

"I don't care if they stare at me," Richard said. "I'm just worried about forgetting the words. It's all words, y'know?"

"Just like comedy," Julia said. "Did you see what happened with that boy Don Potash?"

"The sweat was rolling down his face like a river," Paul said. "I felt sorry for him."

"Me too," said Richard.

"That kid is hilarious, too," Elke said. "He's in my class. He cracks everybody up."

"Poor guy," Paul said. "He's probably traumatized for life."

"What does that mean?" asked Richard.

"It means he can't eat Skittles," Paul said, with a straight face.

"He just froze up," Julia told Richard. "That won't happen to you. You'll remember your lyrics."

"Hey, Raccoon, why don't you just read the words off a paper?" Paul suggested.

"That would be lame," Richard told him. "No rappers read their rhymes. You gotta just rap."

"I get it," Paul said. "Like you made it all up on the spot."

"Yeah," Richard said. "Hey, you're not gonna tell anybody I was scared, are you?"

"Of course not," Elke assured him. "Who would we tell? Your secret is safe with us."

"Hey, speaking of secrets . . . ," Paul whispered.

"Yes?" the others asked, leaning in closer. Nobody can resist a secret.

"I gotta tell you guys something," Paul said. "I'm busting. I can't hold it in anymore."

"What? What? *What?!*"

"The BluffTones are not playing 'Wipeout' in the show," Paul revealed.

"You're *not*?" asked Elke. "Why not?"

"We're tired of it," Paul said. "Anybody can play that song."

"Then why have you been practicing it all week?" asked Julia.

"So the grown-ups will *think* we're gonna play it," Paul told her.

"So what are you gonna play for real?" asked Richard.

"Promise not to tell?" Paul said.

"Cross my heart and hope to die," Richard said.

"If you tell, worms are going to crawl into your body," Paul said. "They'll live in your intestines."

"We won't tell," the others said.

"Okay, here's the secret," Paul whispered. "We're gonna play 'Stacy's Mom.'"

"Get *out*!" Elke said, punching him on the arm.

"It's true," Paul insisted.

The others collapsed into giggles.

"Really?" asked Julia. "Isn't that the song they said you weren't allowed to play?"

"Yup."

"Then why are you going to play it?" asked Julie.

134

"Because we like it," Paul said, "and because we want to stick it to the Man."

"What man?" asked Richard. "Mrs. Marotta isn't a man."

"You know, *the Man*," said Paul. "The grown-ups. The judges. Authority. The censors. People who try to tell you what to do and how to run your life."

"*That's* the Man?" asked Richard.

"You learn fast, Raccoon." said Paul.

"Aren't you worried that you're going to get in trouble?" asked Julia.

"Sure, I'm worried," Paul said. "I'm no rebel. I never did anything like this before."

"Reverend Mercun is going to freak out, you know," Julia said. "He'll probably pull the plug on your amps in the middle of the song."

"Let him," Paul said. "Maybe that will get us on the TV news."

"You won't win the talent show if you do that, you know," Elke pointed out. "They'll disqualify The BluffTones."

"I don't care," Paul replied. "Does it even matter? Everybody knows you're gonna win, anyway."

"That's not true!" Elke protested.

"Oh, please," Paul said. "Sure it's true. You're the most talented kid in town. Everybody knows that."

Elke was about to say something, but she stopped. She looked like she couldn't decide whether or not to tell them something.

"Can I tell *you* guys a secret?" she finally said.

The others leaned forward.

"Go ahead," Julia whispered.

"I don't want to win," Elke said.

"What?" Paul said, flabbergasted. "Are you kidding me? Why not? You'll get that cool car. Even if you can't drive it, you could sell it. It's worth thousands of dollars."

"You're going to be famous, Elke," Julia told her. "Everybody says so. You're going to be the next Justin Chanda."

Elke sighed and shook her head.

"I don't want to be famous," she told them. "My *mom* wants me to be famous. I just want to sing. I love to sing. But I don't want to be a celebrity. I don't want to have people following me around all the time, taking pictures and bothering me. Having to get my hair done all the time. I wish I had your courage, Paul."

"My courage?" Paul said. "What do you mean?"

"You know, the courage to stick it to the Man."

"Who's the Man?" asked Richard.

"My mom is the Man," Elke explained.

"Your mom is a man?" asked Richard.

"No silly," Elke said. "My mom tells me what to do. At least until I'm eighteen."

"So how could you stick it to the man, anyway?" asked Paul.

"I could just not show up," Elke said. "I could ditch the whole talent show. That would show her."

"What?!" Julia said. "Are you serious? Would you actually do that?"

"Maybe," Elke said. "Shhhh. If my mom finds out I'm even thinking about this, she'll kill me."

"It's a bad idea," Paul said, shaking his head. "I hope you won't do that. I'm gonna feel like it's my fault. Like I gave you the idea."

"You didn't," Elke said. "I've been thinking about it for a long time. My mom told me that if I win the talent show, she's going to leave my dad. We're going to take that Hummer and drive to Los Angeles for me to try and make it as a singer and actress."

"Wow," said Richard. "She'd leave your dad if you won?"

"Are you serious?" Julia asked.

"Yes."

"She *told* you that?" Paul asked. "She didn't *ask* you?"

"She *told* me," Elke said, "and I don't want to leave my dad."

"Your mom would actually do that?" Julia asked. "My mom would never force me to do something I didn't want to do."

"My mom wanted to be famous when she was younger," Elke told them. "So when it didn't happen, she decided that she would make *me* famous. I guess it's almost as good."

"So what are you going to do?" Julia asked. "How are you going to tell her you're going to ditch the show?"

"I'm not going to tell her," Elke said. "I'm just not going to show up. I'll send my parents to the show and tell them I'll be there after I walk my dog. Then I won't come. She won't be able to do anything about it."

"She's gonna freak out," Paul said.

"I know," said Elke. "But I can't tell her. Not to her face."

"Why don't you just come to the talent show

and sing bad on purpose?" Richard suggested. "Then you'll lose."

"Not a bad idea, Raccoon," Paul said.

"I can't do that," Elke said. "I wish I could."

It was quiet for a minute while they let it all sink in.

"Hey," Paul finally said, "if Elke ditches the talent show, one of *us* has a good chance to win it. Maybe I should just play 'Wipeout' after all."

"I thought you were so anxious to stick it to the Man," Elke said.

"Oh, yeah," Paul said, snapping his fingers.

"Well, I know one thing for sure," Julia whispered. "My group isn't going to win either way. The Beach Babes are awful."

"If I win," Richard said, "I'm going to sell the car and give the money to *you*, Elke. Because you would have won for sure."

"That's sweet, Richard," Elke said. "But if you win, you keep the prize. You will have earned it."

At that moment, Mrs. Marotta's voice boomed out across the multipurpose room.

"Where is Richard Ackoon?" she hollered. "He's up next! The Beach Babes on deck, and The BluffTones on double deck. Where is Jake

Perelmuter? Coleman Verburg? Let's go, people! This is rehearsal time, not social hour!"

Paul quickly got down on one knee and gathered Elke, Julia, and Richard around him.

"Okay, whatever we said here is secret, right?" he told them. "Nothing leaves this room. Got it?"

The four of them put their hands on top of one another's like a team before the big game.

"Got it."

Chapter 14

A Million-to-One Shot

"Attention. Flight 117 to Los Angeles has been canceled. We regret any inconvenience. . . ."

Justin Chanda was having a *bad* day.

Oh, sure, he was a mega-selling recording artist with millions of fans, three Grammy Awards, his own clothing line, and enough money in the bank that he wouldn't have to work another day in his life. But right now, waiting in line to buy a corn muffin in Tulsa International Airport, none of those things mattered.

After meeting with his lawyer in New York that morning, Justin had been heading back home to California. His connecting flight to Chicago had been diverted to Oklahoma because of bad weather. As he sipped a cup of coffee, he was kicking himself for continuing to fly with commercial airlines instead of buying himself a private jet. He could certainly afford one, and he could have avoided all this mess. *This is what I get for trying to lower my carbon footprint,* he said to himself.

Justin shook his head in disgust. He just wanted to be home.

The day had started poorly, even before he left New York. His girlfriend dumped him. For the past year, Justin had been dating Francesca Wolff, the slinky actress on the hot new TV series *Virtual World*. Just about every week there was another picture of the couple in *People* magazine, frolicking on some beach or shopping in L.A. Then she sent him a text—a *text!*—saying that if he didn't want to marry her, it was all over between them. She said she wanted a man who was willing to make a commitment.

Justin was willing to make a commitment. But not to Francesca Wolff. She was beautiful and they looked great together, but when there were no cameras pointing at them, they simply didn't have much to say to each other. He couldn't imagine spending the rest of his life with somebody like that.

To make the day even worse, Justin's cell phone was dead. He had forgotten to charge it in the hotel room the night before. Living without a cell was almost like living without oxygen.

With his flight canceled, Justin had to figure out what to do next. Hoping to avoid being recognized, he pulled his Dodgers cap down over his eyes and walked over to the DEPARTURES board in the terminal. It was already past four o'clock. There were no more flights to L.A. for the rest of the day.

"Mr. Chanda, can I have your autograph?"

He looked down. It was a girl, probably ten or eleven years old. She was staring up at him like she was looking at Santa Claus. The girl held out a pen and a little autograph book. On one side of the open page, the words "Donald Duck" were written in sloppy handwriting. The girl's parents stood a few feet behind her, beaming under their Mickey Mouse ears.

Justin didn't mind signing *one* autograph. The problem was that if anybody spotted him signing the girl's book, they would come over and ask for an autograph too. And if he was spotted signing for two people, ten more would come over. And if he was seen signing for those ten, a crowd would appear. It always did. Then he might have to sign a *hundred* autographs. He had already signed a bunch for the people on the flight from New York. Justin loved his fans, but writing his name repeatedly on little scraps of paper was the part of celebrity that he could do without.

"Yeah, sure," he told the girl without much enthusiasm. He took the pen and scrawled his name next to Donald's. The girl's mother snapped a photo to preserve the moment.

A men's room was a few yards away, and Justin dashed into it before any other autograph seekers could accost him. He went into a stall, closed the door, and sat down. This was the only place he could be alone and think things over.

Justin reviewed his options. He could see if a nearby airport might have a flight to L.A that night. Or he could stay overnight at a Tulsa hotel and try to catch a flight home to L.A. in the morning. Or, he could rent a car and drive home . . . 1,400 miles. That last option was the least attractive. Plus, it would pump tons of carbon into the atmosphere, which he was opposed to on moral grounds. Just last week he had performed in a benefit concert to save the rainforest.

Justin rooted around in his carry-on bag for his wallet. He would need his credit card and photo ID no matter what he decided to do. While he searched, his fingers came upon a envelope. His lawyer had handed it to him in New York. It was a personal letter. Most of Justin's fan mail was answered by secretaries. But this one came from his hometown, so his lawyer thought it might be important. The return address said "Mary Marotta, Cape Bluff, Kansas."

The name didn't ring a bell. Justin tore the envelope open.

Dear Mr. Chanda,

I don't know if you remember me, but we went to high school together. In fact, you and I were Sandy and Danny in Grease for the senior class play. My last name was Lampert then. Hard to believe ten years have gone by so quickly. Everyone here in Cape Bluff is so proud of what you've accomplished. There's a new principal now, but some of our old teachers are still here, and so is Reverend Mercun, Officer Selleck, and others.

I'm sure you're crazy busy, so I'll get to the point. You probably heard about the tornado ripping up the town. The elementary school library was flooded and almost all the books were ruined. We're holding a talent show at the school on March 21 to raise money and help Cape Bluff get back on its feet. I can't think of anything that would be more inspiring to the kids here than if you were to show up that night and just say hi to everybody.

I know this is a million-to-one shot. But every so often a million-to-one shot comes in. If you can make it, great. If not, the folks of Cape Bluff and I wish you the best of luck with your upcoming projects.

Sincerely,
Mary Marotta (formerly Lampert)

Of *course* Justin remembered Mary Lampert, now Marotta. In fact, he had a crush on her back when they were in high school. He got the lead in *Grease* because he could sing. But he was a skinny little nerd back then and didn't have the courage to ask out such a pretty girl. Mary Lampert dated football players. He didn't think he had a chance with her. Thinking back, he remembered a football player named Marotta. Mary must have married the guy. Lucky guy.

In Justin's mind, he was still a skinny little nerd. But now he was a *rich and famous* skinny little nerd. He was one of the few people who left Cape Bluff and became a success. He had never looked back.

Justin looked at the boarding pass of his canceled flight to check the date—March 21. Then he read Mary's letter again. The talent show was that night.

The grim-faced lady at the United Airlines Customer Service counter took one look at *Chanda, Justin* on the boarding pass, peered at his face, and nearly fainted. Suddenly she was all smiley like a schoolgirl, happy to help him in any way she could. Being a celebrity *does* carry certain advantages.

Justin explained his predicament and the customer service rep pecked some keys on the computer in front of her.

"There's a flight to L.A. tonight from Springfield-Branson Airport," she said, "but that's almost a three-hour drive from here. You'd have to hurry to make it."

"I'll take it," Justin quickly agreed. "I can get there."

He rushed to the rental car area. The lady at the Avis counter also recognized him, and agreed to give him their newest car—a yellow Toyota Prius convertible—in exchange for an autograph.

"Nice!" he said, scrawling his name across a road map on the counter. "A hybrid. Fifty miles to the gallon. Very green. You've got a deal!" He thanked her and hurried to go pick up the car.

Interstate 44 starts near Oklahoma City, passes just below Tulsa, and is a straight shot to Springfield, Missouri. Along the way it crosses the state lines almost exactly where the corners of Kansas, Oklahoma, and Missouri touch.

Justin liked highway driving. He found it relaxing. And having grown up less than two hours from Tulsa, he knew the area. He'd driven it plenty of times.

After an hour or so on I-44, he started to see exit signs for familiar towns—Vinita, Baxter Springs, Joplin. His old stamping grounds. The next sign said CAPE BLUFF, ONE MILE.

Cape Bluff. The old memories came flooding back. He remembered the day he was sitting in the high school cafeteria when he jokingly suggested to his best friend Laurent Linn that they form a bubblegum boy band. Laurent agreed that they couldn't be any worse than The Backstreet Boys or 'N Sync. Justin and Laurent rounded up a few other guys in the school choir and named themselves "Pendulum Dune." The name didn't mean anything, but they thought it sounded cool. Justin wrote a bunch of songs that sounded a lot like those other groups. Laurent was a real techie, and he built a little recording studio in his basement. Pendulum Dune recorded a demo CD there, and sent it to every radio station within a hundred miles. Somehow, it caught the ear of a talent agent who signed the boys to a management deal.

Their debut album, *Swinging with Pendulum Dune*, sold ten million copies and shocked the world. The talent agent ended up stealing all the group's royalties because the boys didn't read the contract carefully. But they had their fifteen minutes of fame, and even got to sing "God Bless America" at a St. Louis Cardinals game.

The other guys in the band were thrilled with their success. But Justin realized that the average career of a boy band lasted one album, maybe two. When he told the group he was leaving, Laurent and the other guys took it hard. They stopped speaking to him. Laurent developed a drinking problem, and only recently kicked it and started up his lighting and sound company.

After Justin left Pendulum Dune, he wrote some rhythm and blues songs, hired a couple of hip-hop producers from L.A., and released a solo album simply titled *Justin Chanda*. It won Best Pop Vocal Album at the Grammy Awards, and Justin was flying high. He started getting small TV and movie parts, opened up a restaurant in West Hollywood, and was named "one of the most stylish men in America" by *GQ* magazine.

It had all started ten years earlier as a joke in the Cape Bluff High School cafeteria. Justin hadn't been back there since.

The Cape Bluff exit was coming up fast on the right side of the highway. Justin pulled over onto the shoulder just before the off-ramp and turned off the engine.

He had a choice to make. He could keep driving to Springfield and catch the flight to L.A. Or, he could pull off at this exit and go to the talent show in Cape Bluff.

It would be great to get back to California that night, and sleep in his own bed. It would also be great to blow everyone's minds by showing up at his old elementary school. He wondered if the house he grew up in had survived the recent tornado.

If he went to the talent show, he knew there were sure to be lots of familiar faces. He wondered if Mary Lampert, that is, Mary *Marotta*, was as pretty as she used to be back in high school. He wondered if Laurent Linn and the guys in Pendulum Dune were still in Cape Bluff, and how they would react if they saw him. Maybe they would ask him for money. Or maybe they would just beat him up for leaving the band to go off and become famous on his own.

He *hated* making these decisions. That's why he had a team of lawyers and agents—to make the tough decisions *for* him. But he couldn't get in touch with them now. His cell phone was dead.

Justin sat in the car at the side of I-44 for a

good fifteen minutes, thinking things over. The sky was looking dark. There was always the chance that the flight from Springfield would be canceled, just like his other flight. Then he would have driven three hours out of his way for nothing. The weather had been really screwy lately.

He sighed, took a deep breath, started up the Prius, and pulled off the highway at the Cape Bluff exit. He would go to the talent show.

He had no idea that this decision was going to change his life.

Chapter 15

A Jumble of Hubbub

An hour before the talent show was scheduled to begin, backstage was a jumble of hubbub and nervous energy. Richard (who by now was being called "The Raccoon" by everybody) was pacing back and forth with his eyes closed, silently rapping his lyrics to himself. Paul and The BluffTones were tuning their electric guitars while working up the nerve to play the forbidden "Stacy's Mom." Somebody's mother was frantically sewing a costume that had ripped at the worst possible moment.

Julia was stretching her quadriceps to release tension, while the other Beach Babes giggled and sent cell phone pictures to their friends, who were sitting in the same room. Jenny and her Sand Kittens warily eyed the Beach Babes from the other side of the stage, being careful not to make eye contact with them.

The Drumming Gorillas beat on their plastic garbage cans to kill the time. Singers practiced their scales. Cheerleaders, jugglers, magicians, ventriloquists, Elvis impersonators, penguin impersonators, and bacon impersonators were milling around waiting for the show to begin. Amy the crochet girl was sitting calmly in the corner—crocheting.

Somebody kept shouting, "Where's my mustache? Has anybody seen my mustache?"

Don Potash, the comedian who suffered from brain freeze and flop sweat during his audition, had felt bad that he would not be part of the show. Two days earlier, he asked Mrs. Marotta if he could help out behind the scenes in some way. She said he could be on the stage crew. Because he was big and strong, Don was assigned the important job of pulling the curtain open and closed for each act.

There was only one performer who wasn't nervously getting ready backstage—Elke Villa. But in all the confusion, nobody noticed she was missing.

The talent show had been switched to the Cape Bluff High School auditorium at the last minute. This was because eight hundred tickets had been sold, and the fire code stated that only five hundred people were allowed in the elementary school multipurpose room at one time. Honest Dave Gale moved the grand prize—the Hummer H3T—over to the front lawn of the high school so everybody could see it when they arrived for the show.

People were still buying tickets at the door and filing into the auditorium thirty minutes before show time. It was going to be standing room only. Three seats in the front row were blocked off with white tape. They were reserved for the judges—Mayor Rettino, Principal Anderson, and Reverend Mercun.

Just about the whole town had come out to see the talent show. At five dollars per ticket, they had raked in at least four thousand dollars from the admissions alone. A lot more money would be made from selling ads in the program, sales of the DVD, still photos of each act, and cupcakes and cookies, which were selling briskly in the lobby.

All that money wouldn't fix the estimated million dollars worth of damage to the school, but it would go a long way toward replacing the library books that had been ruined.

Money talks, as they say. To the grown-ups of Cape Bluff, the talent show was a success before the first act took the stage. Parent volunteers were cheerfully ripping tickets, hawking food, and handing out programs at the door.

"Don't miss the opportunity to buy a DVD of the show!" one usher announced. "You'll have those memories forever. Pick up an order form on the table in the lobby."

"Photos are available for purchase," another volunteer announced. "We have individual action shots, pictures of each act, and a group photo of all our talented performers."

Honest Dave was walking around the audience, schmoozing and hobnobbing with his old customers, new customers, and potential customers. Laurent Linn, the sound and lighting guy, was running around hooking up tiny wireless microphones for the performers so they would be heard.

Mary Marotta was also rushing around, giving quickie pep talks to nervous kids and making sure everyone had the right equipment and costumes. She was almost in a nervous panic herself. There were eight hundred people out there! What if something went wrong? In her eyes, the last rehearsal had pretty much been a disaster, with props breaking, CDs skipping, and kids misbehaving. She really wasn't sure if everything was going to come together in time for the actual show. And she was on the verge of laryngitis from shouting so much at rehearsals.

The media loves heartwarming human interest stories, so *The Cape Bluff Tribune,* Channel 6 Action News, and KNOW-AM "In the Know" radio had sent correspondents to report on the talent show. It was a natural headline: TOWN DEVASTATED BY TORNADO STRUTS ITS STUFF. Tech guys were setting up their equipment and reporters were interviewing parents in the audience.

Most of those parents sat anxiously in their seats. They were hoping their child wouldn't be the one to sing that horrible note, fall off the stage, forget the lyrics, collapse into tears, or humiliate the family in some new and unusual way. Proud grandparents waited patiently for the show to start, some of them having come from hundreds of miles away. Dozens of video cameras were at the ready, fingers hovering over the record button.

Each member of the audience had been instructed to bring along a flashlight with them. It was Mrs. Marotta's idea to end the show with an all-cast sing along and have everybody wave their flashlights back and forth in the dark.

As it got closer to seven o'clock, a buzz of anticipation swept through the audience. Everybody knew the show was about to begin. Mrs. Marotta gathered the kids in the room behind the stage.

"Okay, this is *it*!" she said. "I need to tell you kids something. We all want to be something different from what we are. We all want to be somebody else sometimes. Well, you become someone different when you're on the stage. You each have two minutes to shine in front of the whole town. Show 'em what you've got. Whatever happens out there, I'm proud of you and you should be proud of yourselves. Now let's get this party started."

The doors leading out of the auditorium were closed. The last stragglers found the few remaining seats. The house lights were dimmed. Conversations ended. People shushed their neighbors.

"Pull the curtain, Don!" Mrs. Marotta ordered.

Don Potash pulled open the big curtain and seven Cape Bluff Elementary School teachers were lined up on the stage in size order—wearing old-time bathing suits. Two held beach balls. One had a boogie board. A huge cardboard sun was pinned to the back curtain.

Mrs. Marotta thought it would be fun to get the teachers involved in the talent show, and was amazed that seven of them were willing to do a silly skit to start things off—stripped down in bathing suits, no less.

When the spotlights hit the line of teachers, the crowd roared with laughter and approval. There's nothing funnier than seeing your teacher in a bathing suit. In the front row, Reverend Mercun looked uncomfortable. Nobody told him there would be a skit featuring half-naked teachers.

"Hey y'all, it looks like a good day for surfing!" said Miss Andrews, one of the third grade teachers onstage. She put on a squeaky, high-pitched voice, like she was trying to sound like a teenager.

"Everybody knows the best surfing in the world is right here in Cape Bluff, Kansas," said Mrs. Watson, who taught fourth grade.

"Do you think The Big Kahuna will be coming to the beach today?" asked Mrs. McCarthy, the music teacher.

"Oooh! He's *dreamy!*" gushed Miss Proto, a second-grade teacher.

"Are you kidding?" said Mrs. DiMartino, fifth grade. "That guy is a major creepazoid!"

"Who cares about The Big Kahuna, anyway?" said Miss Katz, the art teacher. "Let's catch some waves!"

Jangly guitars blasted out of the speakers and The Beach Boys started singing, *"If everybody had an ocean across the USA . . ."*

The teachers joined in singing "Surfin' USA," and by the second line the audience was into it, clapping along and stamping their feet. Everybody laughed when the teachers pantomimed surfing or swimming.

When the song came to an end, there was an awkward pause, as if something was supposed to happen next but nobody knew what it was.

Finally, the tip of a surfboard appeared from stage right. The surfboard was on wheels, and it was being pulled across the stage by a rope. A man was standing on it, and when everybody realized it was Principal Anderson, the crowd went crazy, hooting, whistling, and laughing. He was wearing a brightly colored bathing suit, a tie-dyed T-shirt, flip-flops, and on his arms were those inflatable swimmies that parents put on their toddlers who are learning how to swim.

"It's the Big Kahuna!" gushed Miss Proto, and she pretended to faint.

"Cowabunga!" shouted Principal Anderson. "Surf's up, beach bunnies, and I am majorly amped, fer sure! I think I'll shoot the curl and hang ten on those gnarly waves out there. Who's with me?"

The skit was pretty awful, but everyone seemed to enjoy watching the teachers and Principal Anderson make fools of themselves.

While the skit was going on, in the room behind the stage, Mrs. Marotta was looking around at the kids and noticed for the first time that Elke Villa wasn't there.

"Where's Elke?" she asked a boy standing next to her.

"Beats me," he shrugged.

"Has anyone seen Elke?" Mrs. Marotta asked.

All the kids looked around. Nobody had seen Elke.

Mrs. Marotta rushed over and peered through the curtain at the side of the stage. Elke's parents were sitting in the third row. Mrs. Marotta quickly climbed down the steps and into the audience.

"Have you seen Elke?" she whispered to Mrs. Villa.

"She's not backstage?" she replied, concerned. "Elke told us we should come here early to get good seats. She said she was going to walk the dog and then ride her bike over here. But she should have been here by now."

Onstage, the opening skit was finished and Principal Anderson was talking to the audience, welcoming everyone to the talent show.

"Your children and grandchildren have worked *unbelievably* hard preparing for this night," he said. "We're so grateful that you could all come and see the talented boys and girls we have here at Cape Bluff Elementary School. So sit back in your beach chairs, dudes and dudettes, relax, and enjoy the—"

At that moment, the lights went out. The auditorium was plunged into total darkness.

Somebody screamed. There was a buzz of whispered conversation in the audience. It wasn't obvious if this was all part of the show, or what was happening. Flashlights clicked on.

"It's a power outage!" shouted Laurent Linn from the back of the room. "I've got no juice at all!"

The audience murmured with worried restlessness. Somebody handed Principal Anderson a flashlight. He pointed it at his own face and hollered to try to get everyone's attention.

"Okay, calm down, everyone!" he shouted. "Nothing to worry about. I'm sure the lights will be back on in a moment."

Laurent Linn opened the back door of the auditorium and looked outside. The Exxon sign down the street was dark. All the stores on Main Street were dark. The streetlights, too. It was a blackout. The electricity in the whole town of Cape Bluff had been knocked out.

It was still twilight, and the full moon made the sky a little brighter than it normally would be at that hour. In the distance, about two miles away, Mr. Linn could clearly make out something he had seen a number of times before in his life and hoped he would never see again—a dark funnel cloud.

"Not again!" he exclaimed.

Part 3

Chapter 16

The Show Must Go On

The news that another tornado had touched down in Cape Bluff took approximately ten seconds to spread through the packed auditorium. A few seconds later, there was panic in the room. People were yelling out in frustration. Parents were holding their children tightly. Babies were crying. Even *they* sensed something was terribly wrong.

Typically, years and often *decades* would pass between tornadoes hitting Cape Bluff. It was very unusual for two of them to arrive so close together in time.

"Please remain calm, everyone!" Principal Anderson shouted over the sudden worried buzz. "We've all been in this situation before."

"Remain calm?" said Tom Villa, Elke's father, as he jumped up from his seat. "My daughter is out there! I'm going to go find her." Elke's mother had lost control and was sobbing hysterically.

Chief of Police Michael Selleck, sitting two rows behind, got up and grabbed Mr. Villa.

"Tom!" he yelled, wrapping his arms around the big man. "Stop! Don't be crazy!"

"Let me go!"

It took three men to hold Tom Villa back and prevent him from running out of the auditorium to look for Elke.

Lucille Rettino, in the front row, stood up. As mayor of Cape Bluff, she knew it was her responsibility to take control in a crisis situation.

"For safety, we need to stay right here," she announced. "Mike, I'm putting you in charge of finding Elke. Take Mr. Villa and two other men with you. And be careful."

Police Chief Selleck chose a couple of strong men. The four of them grabbed their coats and rushed out the back of the auditorium.

Reverend Mercun rose from his seat and asked if he might say a few words. A hush fell over the audience as he spoke.

"Dear Lord," he prayed. "We ask for no material possessions or wealth or fortune to come to any of us in this room. But we beseech you to protect the life of this young girl. And protect all of us."

"Amen."

A few minutes passed before Honest Dave stood up.

"What are we supposed to do?" he asked. "Just sit here in the dark doing nothing?"

"Yes," Reverend Mercun replied. "Let us sit here in the dark and be thankful that this happened when we are all in this room together. God brought us here for a reason. This room will serve as our shelter, our sanctuary, until the storm blows over."

"What if it blows over *here*?" somebody shouted.

"Let us pray that it doesn't," the reverend replied simply.

People turned off their flashlights. It was quiet for ten minutes or so while some prayed and others worried about what might be happening outside to their homes, their businesses, their farms, their pets, and above all, that poor girl Elke.

The quiet eventually gave way to restlessness and quiet conversations.

"I was just thinking," Principal Anderson said calmly as he stood up. "As long as we're all just sitting here . . . did you ever hear that old saying in show business—the show must go on?"

"How's the show supposed to go on?" asked an old man sitting near him. "I can't even see my hand in front of my face, much less the stage. You're a darn fool, you know that?"

Principal Anderson went to the front of the auditorium and asked the people in the first row to put their flashlights on the edge of the stage and point them toward the curtain. They did. The people in the second row passed *their* flashlights to the people in the first row, who put those flashlights on the stage also. The people in the third row saw what was happening, and they got up to pass *their* flashlights forward too.

And then, like a wave, hundreds of flashlights were passed to the front of the auditorium, where the people in the first row put them into position. The effect was not quite as bright as one strong spotlight, but the stage was surprisingly well illuminated by a bright beam of light.

Mrs. Marotta came out to center stage, getting a nice round of applause.

"It looks like we're going to be here for a while," she said. "We're all praying for Elke's safety. But Mr. Anderson is right. The show must go on!"

"Yeah!" shouted all the kids backstage.

When the cheer came out of the crowd, Mrs. Marotta went behind the curtain and gathered the kids around her.

"Okay," she said, "we've got light, but no electricity. That means no CD player. If your act depended on recorded music, you're going to have to improvise. Any amplifiers are useless, so forget about those electric guitars, boys. Drum machines too, Raccoon. Oh, and our microphones won't work either. You're going to have to project your voices."

"How can we—," somebody started.

"This is show biz, kids," Mrs. Marotta told them. "And this is life, too. You never know what's going to hit you. Sometimes life throws unexpected stuff at you, and you've got to deal with it."

She looked at her clipboard with all the acts listed on it and made a quick decision to juggle the lineup. Piano and violin players would go on first, because they didn't need any electricity or amplification. With a little luck, the tornado would miss the center of town and power would come back on quickly, so the acts that needed to plug in would be able to go on as planned. Everybody scurried backstage and Mrs. Marotta signaled Don Potash to pull open the curtain for the first act.

Jimmy, the quiet little third grader, came out with his violin to a big round of applause and played Beethoven's "Violin Sonata #7 in C Minor." The audience loved it. When he was done, Don pulled the curtain closed, and the judges made some notes on the score sheets in front of them.

Jimmy was followed by a girl playing Mozart's "Piano Concerto #21 in C major." The crowd gave her warm applause. Then there were the Irish step dancers, Abbott and Costello, the juggler, the magician, Ricky the bacon impersonator, the accordionist, a mime, a poet, Amy the crochet girl, the unicyclist, and The Janitors, who threw dirt all over the stage and swept it up, to the amusement of the audience.

When The Drumming Gorillas hit the stage, nobody knew what to expect, least of all The

Drumming Gorillas. They started beating on their garbage cans haphazardly at first, and the crowd had a good laugh. The boys started watching one another as they drummed, and then gradually settled on a regular beat. None of them had ever played drums before, but they must have had some innate sense of rhythm, because soon they were improvising and sounding like they actually knew what they were doing. The crowd began to clap to the beat and stamp their feet. Encouraged, The Drumming Gorillas started banging their heads against their garbage cans, their garbage cans against the floor, and finally against one another. When they were done, they received a huge round of applause. Not bad for a bunch of guys who had never performed anything in their lives before, and didn't even want to be *in* the talent show.

Backstage, the kids who needed electricity for their acts were scrambling to figure out what to do. Raccoon, who always rapped along with his drum machine, would have to keep the beat some other way. Paul took him down the hall to the music room, where they found an old wind-up metronome Raccoon could use. While they were in there, Paul spotted three acoustic guitars in a closet. Perfect. It would be The BluffTones *unplugged*.

While the early acts were onstage, Mrs. Marotta gathered the Beach Babes and Sand Kittens around her. Both groups were lip synch dance acts, and entirely dependent on recorded music.

"Can any of you sing?" Mrs. Marotta asked.

"No."

"Can any of you dance without your music?" she asked.

"We can't even dance *with* our music!" admitted one of the Sand Kittens, causing the other girls to collapse in giggles.

"Julia can dance," Anne said.

Everybody turned and looked at Julia.

"I just do a little ballet," she said shyly. "I'm not very good."

"Would any of you girls mind if Julia were to dance solo?" asked Mrs. Marotta.

"But I . . . I can't . . . not by myself," Julia protested. "I don't have my pointe shoes. I don't have—"

"Oh, come on, Julia!" urged Anne. "You can do it."

"You're really good!" said Chloe.

"You're the only one of us who can dance anyway," said Caroline.

"We need some acts, Julia," Mrs. Marotta told her. "It's not much of a talent show if we just have a bunch of guys dressed as gorillas banging on garbage cans."

"Please?" Anne begged.

Everyone was looking at her.

"Well . . . ," Julia finally said, "okay. I'll do it."

"That's the spirit!" Mrs. Marotta said, clapping her on the back. "Get out there and strut your stuff."

Don pulled open the curtain. Julia ran out to the center of the stage on tiptoe, hundreds of flashlights shining up at her.

In the audience, her parents gasped. So did Anne's parents and Sergei Propopotov, the Russian choreographer. What happened to the Beach Babes and Sand Kittens?

It was *good* that Julia didn't have time to prepare and practice for this moment. Because that also meant she didn't have time to worry and doubt her ability. She had made the snap decision to perform *The Dying Swan*, a solo dance that was created in 1905 by the Russian choreographer Mikhail Fokine for the ballerina Anna Pavlova. It was only a few minutes long, and Julia's class had been working on it at ballet school the previous week.

The crowd settled to a hush as Julia spun around to face the rear of the stage. Still on tiptoe, she raised her arms and began undulating them up and down slowly. It looked like a swan flapping its wings.

On the sides of the stage, the other performers watched intently. Most of the kids at school didn't even know Julia took ballet lessons.

"Is she doing *The Dying Swan*?" whispered Jimmy, the little third-grade violin player as he stood next to Mrs. Marotta.

"I believe so," she whispered back. "It's beautiful, isn't it?"

"I know the song that goes with it," Jimmy said. "It's from *Le Carnival des Animaux*."

"Well, play it," Mrs. Marotta told him. "*Play* it!"

Jimmy lifted his violin to his chin and drew his bow across the strings. Julia, hearing the familiar notes of *The Dying Swan*, pushed the eight hundred people in the audience out of her head and got lost in the music. She circled the stage slowly, dreamily, gliding with precise footwork while moving her arms elegantly and expressively, like a light and delicate swan coming down for a landing. Every person in the audience watched, silent and spellbound.

Julia's legs were quivering, not out of nervousness, but because the swan is so fragile. As the title suggests, it is dying, but struggling to live. Julia took a series of faltering steps toward the edge of the stage and then sank to her knees, her arms still undulating gracefully behind her back. She rose for a minute to fly, but then collapsed, her fingers trembling as she bowed her head against one knee and grasped her feet in a final, sorrowful death.

The audience exploded in a spontaneous standing ovation.

Don pulled the curtain closed. Julia got up and skipped offstage, a wide grin on her face. It was the first time she had ever performed by herself, and the audience *loved* her. They were on their feet for her. She went out for another bow, and felt a surge of confidence all over her body.

It was Raccoon's turn. Don opened the curtain,

and when they saw him, Raccoon's third-grade classmates let out a roar.

"Yo," he said, winding up the metronome and putting it down on the stage in front of him. "I need a beat, y'all."

Raccoon snapped his fingers with the metronome, which prompted the audience to begin snapping their fingers with him. Eight hundred people were snapping their fingers. Raccoon began to rap:

You rappers, you homies, you California fools
I hear you got your problems. Let me take you all to school.

It seems like all you do, is whimper and complain.
Am I supposed to cry because you got a little rain?

You think you got it bad. Well, I think you got it good.
Maybe you should come and see my Kansas neighborhood.

Cape Bluff is the name of the town where I reside.
I know you never heard of it. But we got lots of pride.

It happened not too long ago when some of us were napping.
Some of us were singing, and one of us was rapping.

The Talent Show

The point I wanna make is we were minding our own business.
Nobody had a clue 'bout what we would shortly witness.

My dad was in the field. He was raking.
He was hoeing.
The sky got dark and gloomy and the wind it started blowing.

He got down on his knees to pull up a potato.
And when he looked up in the air he saw a big tornado.

The kids all started screaming. So did their Ma's and Pa's.
I thought it was a remake of The Wizard of Oz.

It swept right through the town, wrecking everything in sight.
The air was filled with garbage, the day was turned to night.

I staggered. I fell. And then I almost hurled.
Outside it looked like it could be the end of the world.

Everything we had was gone, even my PlayStation.
I bet in your whole life you never seen such devastation.

And then it was over. There was stillness in the air.
People walking around saying how it wasn't fair.

You think we called it quits. You think we've had enough?
Well, homies, you don't know the people of Cape Bluff.

I lived here all my life. This is a very special town.
And believe me, no tornado is gonna keep us down.

It took its best shot, but you should never say never.
'Cause we are gonna come back stronger than ever!

When it was over, Raccoon's parents were crying. They had never heard their son rap before. It was at that moment that they realized Richard wasn't some gangsta like those rappers on TV. He was a *poet*.

The audience rose to give Raccoon a huge ovation, and Don pulled the curtain closed. Mrs. Marotta signaled to Paul that it was time for The BluffTones to go on. Paul and the band hustled to carry Victor's drums onstage. Even though they didn't have electric guitars and amps to worry about, it still takes some time just to set up a drum set. In addition to the drums, Victor had a crash cymbal, a ride cymbal, and a hi-hat, and he was very particular about the way they were positioned.

Don was about to open the curtain, but Mrs. Marotta stopped him.

"They're not ready!" she shouted. "Hang on!"

Don was standing out on the stage, waiting for The BluffTones to finish setting up their drums.

"You rock, Potash!" somebody yelled from the audience.

"Tell a joke, Donnie Boy!" yelled somebody else.

Don looked off to the side, where Mrs. Marotta was standing.

"Go ahead," she said, "tell 'em a joke."

Don looked out at the audience. The first joke that popped into his head was the first joke he ever heard.

"What's pink and fluffy?" he asked.

"What?" replied the audience as one.

"Pink fluff!"

Everybody laughed.

"Tell another one!" somebody yelled.

Don looked toward Mrs. Marotta again. She could see that behind the curtain The BluffTones were having trouble adjusting the foot pedal to the bass drum. She gave Don the "stretch" sign, and nodded her head encouragingly.

Don could have told a few of the jokes from the comedy notebook he had been compiling for years. But instead, he thought back to the routine he had written about the stuff on his desk at home, the routine he couldn't remember at his audition. Suddenly, it all came back.

"Well, the theme to our talent show is the beach," Don began. "I don't know about you folks, but when I think of the beach I think of summer. And you know what I think of when I think of summer?"

"What?" somebody yelled.

"School supplies," Don said.

Laughter. *Nobody* thinks of school supplies when they think of summer.

"No, really!" Don continued. "Because just before school starts, they send you this long list of school supplies you need to buy. Nice way to tell us summer's over, huh?"

That got a good-natured laugh from the kids in the crowd.

"We have to buy rulers and loose-leaf paper and book covers and pens and pencils and glue sticks," Don went on. "That's a big choice, you know. You have to decide between glue sticks, Elmer's glue, or Krazy Glue. That's the decision that keeps me up at night. Hey, I have a question for you guys. Is Elmer's glue made from cows?"

"No," somebody hollered.

"Then why do they have a cow on the label?" Don asked. "Man, cows are amazing animals. They give us milk. They give us hamburgers and steaks. And they even give us glue. That's what I call multitasking."

The crowd was tittering, so Don continued.

"I prefer Krazy Glue myself. That stuff must stick really well because their logo is a guy wearing a hard hat, and he's hanging from the letter *A* in 'Krazy.' His hat is stuck to the letter *A!* Gotta buy *that* stuff. You never know when you might be at school and have to stick your hat to a giant letter and hang there. I had no idea that going to school could be so dangerous."

"How dangerous is it?" somebody hollered.

"I'll tell you how dangerous it is," Don replied. "I'm always having accidents at school. Y'know, paper cuts and stuff. The fumes from those felt-tipped markers. That stuff can make you pass out! And I almost blinded myself with my own laser pointer in third grade. Hey, one time I closed a loose-leaf binder on my finger. Ever do that? Man, that *hurts*. Another school supply–related injury. I tell you, those things should come with warning labels."

While the audience was chuckling, Don looked over at Mrs. Marotta. The BluffTones had finished adjusting their drums and were ready to play, but she didn't want to tell Don that. The audience was really enjoying him.

"Keep going," she said. "Keep going!"

"I stapled my finger once," Don told the crowd. "Did you ever do that? There was a staple sticking in my *finger*! Hey, speaking of Staples, I gotta tell you a little secret. Up until recently, I thought that all they sold at Staples was *staples*. I thought, what a dumb idea for a store to just sell staples. I didn't even think they sold staplers. Just staples. I figured, how often does anybody need to buy staples? Once every few *years*? I kept thinking, what keeps this store in business? Then my mom took me to Staples to get school supplies. I looked around at all the stuff. A guy came over and asked if I needed any help, so I said, 'where are the staples?' The guy said, 'Sorry, we're out of staples.'"

That got a big laugh.

"So anyway, I'm in Staples," Don said, "and when you walk in the door the first thing you see is an aisle full of sticky notes. A whole *aisle*! They've got ten different sizes, different colors, different shapes. They got flags or flowers on some of them. Some of them are scented. They've got *super* sticky ones. Some are lined, or they come in a little plastic cube. They even sell a highlighter that comes with built-in sticky notes. Okay, I *get* it. Do we really need that many options when it comes to our sticky note needs?"

Don was in a groove now. The crowd was eating it up. Even some of the grown-ups in the audience were wiping their eyes. It was a rush. He had them in the palm of his hand. He was improvising now. He hadn't even thought anything else out in advance.

"Hey, what's the deal with Wite-Out?" he said. "My mom told me that before they had computers, students corrected their mistakes with Wite-Out. Can you believe that? She showed me some of her old school papers. It's like, gee, the teacher won't notice the mistake I made because it's covered by a BIG, WHITE, SPLOTCH. How dumb were teachers back in those days?"

He looked over at Mrs. Marotta. She was laughing and gesturing for him to keep going.

"Y'know what else they sell at Staples?" he said. "They sell those little gold stars and stickers that teachers put on your homework when you do a good job. *'Ohhh, look Mommy, I got a STICKER!'* Who do the teachers think they're fooling with those dumb stickers? I say when we do a good job on our homework, they should pay us in *cash.* I'd try a lot harder for cash. Wouldn't you? Those stickers are worthless. You can buy like a hundred of 'em at Staples for a buck ninety-nine. That totally burst my bubble. I tell you, Staples can really rob you of your innocence."

Mrs. Marotta flashed Don the okay sign.

"I'd like to discuss something that's near and dear to me," Don told the crowd. "Pencil sharpeners. But I think our next act is ready. So, continuing with the beach theme, our very own Cape Bluff rock group is going to play 'Wipeout.' Give it up for The BluffTones!"

The crowd erupted in a huge round of applause. It wasn't for The BluffTones. It was for *him.* Don had never felt so *alive*. He made a deep bow and pulled open the curtain.

Paul took a deep breath and looked out at the audience. He spotted his father in the fifth row and winked at him. Then he looked at his bandmates, nodded his head, and began to sing.

> *Stacy's mom has got it going on . . .*
> *Stacy's mom has got it going on . . .*

For a moment, the audience just sat there, confused. *That's not "Wipeout"!* Everybody knows "Wipeout" starts with a drum solo.

> *Stacy can I come over after school.*
> *We can hang around by the pool . . .*

And then, as the judges finally realized what was happening, Reverend Mercun tried to get up from his seat and stop the song. Mayor Rettino put her arm up to grab his jacket, and he sat back down. Looking around, he could see that heads in the audience were bobbing up and down, toes were tapping, and some kids were even dancing in the aisles. Reverend Mercun sat stone-faced until the song was over.

I know it might be wrong but I'm in love with Stacy's mom.

Paul and The BluffTones took a quick bow and hustled off the stage as if they had a plane to catch.

"Ha!" Paul yelled to the rest of the band as they slapped one another on the back. "That'll show 'em!"

"Do you think we'll get kicked out of school?" Victor asked. But Paul couldn't hear him because the cheering was so loud. He had never had so much fun in his life.

The BluffTones had played the forbidden "Stacy's Mom," and the world hadn't fallen off its axis. No innocent children were corrupted. Life went on.

Mrs. Marotta went out to center stage.

"Well, that was . . . a surprise," she said.

She introduced the remaining acts one at a time. Some of them were flat-out terrible. Others that started with next to nothing at their audition came together, and some were surprisingly good. But all of them, even the worst performers, had a feeling of accomplishment when it was over. They had stepped up on a stage and sang, danced, pounded a garbage can, or did *something* they weren't used to doing. It takes courage for anybody to do that.

And each of those kids, having faced that challenge and overcome it, was a stronger person after it was all over. The entire Cape Bluff community could feel it as they rose to give one more round of applause to the kids. They knew that if you can face one challenge, you're better equipped to handle the next one. Those kids had pulled the whole town together.

When the last act had left the stage, Mayor Rettino, Principal Anderson, and Reverend Mercun put their heads together and discussed their scores in whispered voices. While they were working on their decision, Honest Dave climbed up on the stage with a bouquet of flowers and presented it to Mrs. Marotta as a gift for all the hard work she had put into making the talent show a success. The only thing that could have made it better, he said, would have been if Elke Villa had been able to sing.

Involuntarily, the audience turned around and looked at the back door, as if it was about to open and Elke would walk in. But the door remained stubbornly shut.

The three judges were taking a long time to reach a decision. The audience was buzzing with people trying to predict the winner. Most of them seemed to think it was between Julia, the ballet dancer, and Raccoon, the rapper. The BluffTones might have won, but they probably disqualified themselves by playing "Stacy's Mom." Of course, there was always the chance that the judges would pick Jimmy the violin player or even The Drumming Gorillas. There was some casual betting going on within the crowd.

"Julia! Julia! Julia!" some of the girls started to chant.

"Raccoon! Raccoon! Raccoon!" countered some of Raccoon's friends.

"*All* of these kids are winners if you ask me," Mrs. Marotta said, holding her fingers in a *V* to quiet the crowd. "But judges, have you reached a decision?"

"We have," said Mayor Rettino.

"And what have you decided?"

"The winner of the Cape Bluff Elementary School's talent show is . . . Don Potash!"

Well, Don Potash just about passed out. He wasn't even supposed to be *in* the talent show, but his comedy routine turned out to be the winner.

Honest Dave went over and handed Don the keys to the Hummer. A bunch of boys picked Don up and carried him around the auditorium like he was a king. It had been some night.

But it wasn't over yet.

Chapter 17

Avis Is Not Gonna Be Happy

Seconds after Justin Chanda pulled the Prius convertible off Interstate 44, he spotted something out the corner of his eye—a funnel-shaped cloud.

"Holy—"

He had seen one tornado in his life, as a young boy. It had touched down briefly in the outskirts of Cape Bluff, but didn't do much damage before moving on. This one looked bigger, darker, more dangerous. Or maybe it just seemed that way because he was older now, and had more to lose.

The tornado looked like it was about a mile away, hovering over the center of the town, not moving left or right. After he got past his initial surprise, Justin quickly went into survival mode and began to formulate a strategy.

He looked in the rearview mirror. There was no way to turn around and get back on the highway. All the cars were heading the other direction, jamming the ramp onto the I-44.

He pounded the steering wheel. *I never should have pulled off the highway,* he scolded himself. *I should have gone straight to the airport.*

He also kicked himself for not checking the weather report before he left. But it wouldn't have made a difference anyway. Tornadoes sometimes just pop up out of nowhere without warning.

It was getting dark. Justin glanced at his watch. He didn't remember what time the talent show was supposed to begin.

It was starting to rain. *Why in the world did I rent a convertible?* he asked himself. One bad decision after another. There had to be a way to put the top up. Justin punched every button, twisted every dial, and pulled every lever he could reach. He did eventually find the latch that raised the hood. It went up about six inches and then stopped. Jammed. *Great.*

He flipped on the radio. Maybe it would tell

him which direction the tornado was heading. Static came out of the speakers. Ambulances and fire trucks were zipping by on both sides, sirens blaring. It was dangerous. Justin didn't want to take his eyes off the road to fiddle with the radio. He kept his hands on the wheel.

This could be a public relations disaster for me, it occurred to him. If he drove in the opposite direction of the tornado and anybody found out, the press would say he was a coward. If he drove toward the tornado, the press would call him stupid. And if he got caught in the middle of the tornado, well, the press might call him dead.

Hmmm, dying might be a good career move, he thought. Die young, leave a good-looking corpse. It worked for Elvis. He never got old. It worked for Jimi Hendrix, Jim Morrison, James Dean, Marilyn Monroe—

No, don't be a fool.

Justin wasn't thinking straight. This was the time to make smart decisions. And the only choices were bad ones.

Looking in the distance, there was something almost *beautiful* about the tornado. It enveloped the whole sky for miles, with a small whitish funnel hanging down and getting progressively narrower as it got closer to the ground. Power lines in the distance were sparking from the lightning strikes. It was mesmerizing. Justin found it hard to keep the car on the road, because he just wanted to stare at the sky.

The road, Pompton Turnpike, ran east-west alongside Cape Bluff. Justin didn't have a sense that he was driving toward the tornado, but it appeared to be slightly larger in his field of view.

He struggled to remember what he was told back in elementary school during all those tornado drills. If you see a twister in the distance and it's not moving to the right or left relative to trees or telephone poles, it may be moving toward you.

Great.

If the tornado was moving toward him, it could be going as fast as seventy miles per hour. Or faster. It could catch him and sweep him up in its path.

He remembered one piece of advice he used to hear all the time. If you're in a car and you see a tornado coming toward you, get *out*. Take shelter. It's tempting to try and outrun it, but a tornado can pick your car up like a Matchbox toy and heave it into the next county. The best thing to do is get out and lay in a ditch.

The average person will heed that advice. There are three kinds of people who won't. Really stupid people, for one. Crazy people, for another. And the third kind of person is someone who is wildly successful at everything they do.

Someone like Justin Chanda.

From a very early age, Justin seemed to lead a charmed life. He had never failed at anything important. He got rich and famous very quickly. Everything he ever tried worked out. Every risk he ever took paid off. He had no reason to think it would be any different now.

I can outrun a tornado, he decided. Jamming his foot on the accelerator, he pushed it to the floor and the Prius bolted forward.

At the Villa house, the search party arrived with flashlights and axes. The house was fine. The tornado hadn't touched the block.

"Elke!" her father shouted desperately as he ran in the door. "You in here, sweetheart?"

No answer. Her bicycle wasn't in the garage either. Mr. Villa feared the worst. She was out on the street somewhere.

Meanwhile, Justin Chanda's speedometer had nosed past seventy miles per hour. Flecks of mud were hitting his windshield now, and slapping him in the face too. He fumbled for the wiper switch. He could see the tornado looming in all three of his rearview mirrors. It looked almost like it was following him.

There weren't many other drivers on the road, but the ones who were out there appeared to have forgotten everything they learned in driver's ed class. Red lights and stop signs no longer mattered. People were driving full throttle on sidewalks and even lawns. Nobody was using turn signals. Some of them were trying to get away from the path of the tornado. Others were crazies who liked to chase tornadoes and shoot video of them up close.

A blue SUV with some teenagers inside sideswiped Justin's Prius and then veered off into a fire hydrant, sending a geyser of water high in the air. It was a free-for-all. Every man for himself. The few people outside were running for their lives. It was not a good night to be out on the streets.

A bolt of lightning lit up the sky. The wind was picking up. It was getting nasty. Justin tightened his grip on the steering wheel and squinted to see the road in front of him. His ears were popping from the change in air pressure. He told himself that he would gladly give up his gold records—*all* of them—to be in California right now. Back home, all he had to worry about were mudslides, wildfires, earthquakes, and agents. But not tornadoes.

He was doing eighty miles per hour in a thirty-five mile per hour zone, but the tornado was still closing from behind. Debris was flying around and slamming into the back of the Prius. He had to get off this road. Get indoors.

Justin made a screeching turn onto a local street, which forced him to slow down. He tried to remember his Cape Bluff geography. *Where's the old elementary school?* Everything looked so different. A lot can change in ten years. It was hard to read the street signs in the dark.

He was a few blocks from the school when he heard a roar and saw a pig—*a pig!*—come flying out of the sky and crash in the backseat of the Prius. He was chauffeuring a pig around! He almost wet his pants.

When he turned around to get a good look at the pig, the funnel was right behind the car. Debris was flying everywhere. The roar of the wind hurt his ears.

He stepped on the gas again, urging the little car to go faster. There was junk scattered all over the road. Justin prayed that he wouldn't run over anything sharp and pop the tires. That would be the end of this joyride.

Suddenly, he saw something at the side of the road that made him slam on the brakes. It was a bicycle. On top of the bicycle was a huge branch that had just about crushed it.

And next to the bike was a girl.

She was lying on her side, clutching her leg with one hand and a small dog with the other.

It was Elke.

She was crying and calling for help. The Prius screeched to a stop and Justin jumped out. He wasn't sure if he should pick her up. When people get a spinal cord injury, he knew, it's important not to move them.

"Are you okay?" Justin shouted over the roar as he knelt over Elke. Her face was streaked with sweat, dirt, and tears. She held her dog tightly and nodded her head. The dog was soaking wet and looked terrified too.

Elke wiped her face with her sleeve, looked up at Justin, and a second or two later, her mouth dropped open.

"Aren't you . . . Justin Chanda?" she shouted. "The singer?"

"Yeah!"

"What are you doing *here*?"

"I was on my way to a talent show!" he shouted back.

"Me too!" yelled Elke. "I wanted to walk my dog Lucky first!"

"Come on, let's go together," Justin shouted. "We'll bring your dog with us. Can you walk?"

"I don't think so," Elke groaned, testing to see if she could put weight on her leg. "My leg might be broken."

No time to think. He scooped her up in his

arms and carried Elke and Lucky to the Prius. The pig had already jumped out and was limping away. It had wisely decided that the backseat of a convertible was not the safest place to be in a tornado.

"You a singer too?" Justin asked as he carefully put Elke and Lucky into the front passenger seat.

"Yeah, a little."

Another branch fell from the tree and almost landed on the car.

"How do we get to the elementary school from here?" Justin shouted at Elke.

"The show is at the high school!" she shouted back. "They changed it. It's just two blocks away."

Justin pushed the starter button, but the Prius didn't start. He tried again. Nothing. A brick came flying out of the sky and slammed into the hood, denting it.

"Come on!" he shouted at the car as he pounded the steering wheel.

"Why are you driving a convertible?" Elke yelled.

Justin didn't answer. He jumped out of the Prius, ran around the other side, opened the passenger door, and scooped up Elke and Lucky again. They would have to go the rest of the way on foot. The wind was ripping at their clothes and hair.

"Which way?" he shouted in Elke's ear.

The roar of the tornado, right behind them, was impossible to speak over. She pointed, and Justin struggled to carry her and the dog.

He made it halfway down the street when there was a *whoosh*ing sound behind them. Justin turned around just in time to see the tip of the funnel touch down right over the Prius. And then, as if by magic, the car started to rise up off the ground.

"Holy—"

They could only stare. The car began spinning clockwise as it got sucked up into the funnel of the tornado like a dust bunny into a vacuum cleaner. And then, the Prius was *gone*.

"Did you see *that*?" Elke yelled, not sure if she could believe her own eyes.

"Avis Rent-A-Car is not gonna be happy," Justin yelled back.

He turned the corner onto Maplewood Road. Elke and Lucky were not heavy, but there's no easy way to carry a girl and a dog two blocks. The high school was in sight now, and Justin picked up the pace.

"Why is there a car in front of the school?" he asked as he struggled up the front steps.

"That's the grand prize for the talent show," she told him. "It's a Hummer."

"But kids can't—"

He didn't finish the sentence because Elke let out a scream so close to his ear that he almost dropped her. She was looking up in the sky behind him.

Justin turned around and looked up too. A large object was coming down, almost, it appeared, in slow motion. It looked like it might land on top of them.

"What's that!?" Elke yelled.

"That's my car!"

"Watch out!"

The rented Prius turned over once in the air, so its roof was facing the ground. And then, with a huge crash, it landed—on top of the Hummer—crushing it. Justin and Elke covered their eyes so they wouldn't get hit by flying glass.

"Something tells me we're still in Kansas," he told her.

The sound of a Toyota Prius landing on top of the Hummer was not heard inside the auditorium, because everyone in there was still cheering. The talent show had just ended. Don Potash was being carried around on the shoulders of his friends.

Outside, Justin was pounding repeatedly on the auditorium door with his fist.

"Open up!" he shouted.

Finally, the person closest to the door, Laurent Linn, heard the pounding and went to open it.

"Who is it?" he hollered.

"Justin Chanda."

"Very funny."

Laurent opened the door and stared at Justin and Elke, openmouthed. He hadn't seen his old bandmate since Pendulum Dune broke up almost ten years ago.

"Sorry we're late," Justin said.

"What are *you* doing here?" asked Laurent.

"Mary Lampert . . . uh . . . Marotta invited me," he replied. "Can we come in, please? It's been a rough night."

It was only then that Laurent noticed that Justin was holding a girl in his arms, and the girl was holding a dog in *her* arms.

"She's back!" he shouted. "Elke is back!"

When word got around that Elke was safe and that Justin Chanda had returned to Cape Bluff, everybody in the room went crazy. People rushed to tend to Elke, while Justin was hustled up to the front of the auditorium and brought up on stage, where Mary Marotta was holding her flowers.

"I can't believe you actually showed up!" the wide-eyed Mrs. Marotta told Justin.

"You invited me, Mary," he replied. "Did you think a little tornado was going to keep me away?"

"You're a mess!" she said, brushing a leaf out of his hair.

"You look as pretty as you did in high school," he replied.

She blushed. When they were in high school, he had never commented on her appearance. Aside from being in the senior class play together, they had barely spoken back then. And certainly, she had never been told she looked great by a celebrity. She didn't know what to say. So she changed the subject.

"The show is over," she finally whispered in his

ear. "But would you be willing to sing a song, or maybe say a few words?"

Justin turned around. The crowd was on its feet, and a chant was making its way across the auditorium.

"Chanda! Chanda! Chanda!"

Justin turned to Mary.

"That little girl missed the talent show," he told her. "She told me she's a singer. Do you think she would sing with me?"

In the audience, the school nurse was cleaning Elke up and tending to her wounds. It didn't look like her leg was broken, but someone had been dispatched to the nurse's office to get a pair of crutches anyway. Mary Marotta jumped off the stage and went to whisper something in Elke's ear. With a little urging from her mother, Elke was brought up on stage with Justin.

"Elke! Elke! Elke!" chanted the crowd.

"Will you sing a song with me?" Justin whispered in her ear.

"I was going to do 'Over The Rainbow,'" she replied. "Key of C."

"That works for me."

The crowd got quiet and believe me, those two

sang just about the prettiest a cappella version of "Over The Rainbow" that has ever been sung. By the second verse, everybody was holding up flashlights and waving their arms back and forth.

And just after they finished the last line of the song—*If happy little bluebirds fly beyond the rainbow, why, oh, why can't I?*—the lights in the auditorium flickered back on.

The kids . . .

- **Elke Villa** toured the world the next summer as one of the backup singers for Justin Chanda. He is now producing her first solo album. Her parents stayed together.

- **The BluffTones** were not kicked out of school. They got a few birthday party gigs after the talent show, but split up the next year due to "creative differences." The other boys gave up music, but Paul Crichton plans to attend Berklee College of Music in Boston.

- **Julia Maguire** became the top dancer at The Fontaneau Ballet Studio the next year, and performed as a solo in *A Midsummer Night's Dream*. She wants to become a ballet teacher.

- **Richard ("Raccoon") Ackoon** decided to give up rap music and become a poet. He is working on self-publishing his first batch of poems in book form.

- **Don Potash** began to write jokes and scripts and send them to famous comedians. His goal is to become a writer for *Saturday Night Live*.

The grown-ups . . .

- **Honest Dave Gale** gave another Hummer to Don Potash after the first one was crushed. Then he sold all the Hummers in his lot at bargain prices, closed down Hummer Heaven for three months, and reopened as Honest Dave's Hybrid Heaven.

- **Laurent Linn** was hired by Justin Chanda to do the lighting and sound for his worldwide tour.

- **Mary Marotta** got the acting bug again. A local theater company was holding auditions for a production of *The Music Man*, and Mary tried out. She got the role of Marion the Librarian.

- **Justin Chanda** donated a million dollars to repair the damage to Cape Bluff Elementary

School and fill the library with new books. The day after the talent show, he called up Mary Marotta and asked her if she would like to have dinner with him that night. She said yes.

Did you **LOVE** this book?

Want to get access to great books for **FREE?**

Join

Simon & Schuster IN THE **bookloop**

where you can

✗ Read great books for FREE! ✗

Get exclusive excerpts

Chat with your friends

Vote on polls

Log on to everloop.com
and join the book loop group!

MYSTERY. ADVENTURE. HOMEWORK.

ENTER THE WORLD OF DAN GUTMAN.

PUBLISHED BY SIMON & SCHUSTER
BOOKS FOR YOUNG READERS
KIDS.SIMONANDSCHUSTER.COM

I'm a good kid.[1] But when my parents dragged me to a family camp,[2] I decided it was time to totally reinvent myself as a whole new person. But new identities come with lots of new trouble.[3]

anyway*

A STORY ABOUT ME WITH 138 FOOTNOTES, 27 EXAGGERATIONS, AND 1 PLATE OF SPAGHETTI

ARTHUR SALM

---

[1] But not so good that it's going to make you sick to read about me.

[2] Not that I had a choice. I mean, I'm twelve, right?

[3] No room to tell you here. Read the book!

EBOOK EDITION ALSO AVAILABLE
From Simon & Schuster Books for Young Readers
KIDS.SimonandSchuster.com

STEVE BRIXTON is AMERICA'S next great KID DETECTIVE

(whether he wants to be or not)....

"Action! Adventure! Humor!
Mac Barnett has written a book kids will devour."
—Jeff Kinney, author of *Diary of a Wimpy Kid*

EBOOK EDITIONS ALSO AVAILABLE

KIDS.SimonandSchuster.com

FROM SIMON & SCHUSTER BOOKS FOR YOUNG READERS